Andalusia Forest

THE CURSE AT TORRENS FALLS

Mary Ann Poll

America's Lady of Supernatural Thrillers

We don't want to change the laws.
We want to publish the books.
"Evan Swensen"

PUBLICATION
CONSULTANTS
WE BELIEVE IN THE POWER OF AUTHORS

PO Box 221974 Anchorage, Alaska 99522-1974
books@publicationconsultants.com, www.publicationconsultants.com

ISBN Number: 978-1-63747-057-2
eBook ISBN Number: 978-1-63747-085-5
Audio ISBN Number: 978-1-63747-191-3

Library of Congress Catalog Card Number: 2023946872

Manufactured in the United States of America

Dedication

To Dwayne, whose encouragement and support are the reasons my dream of being an author was realized.

ACKNOWLEDGMENTS

Many thanks to my treasured friend and mentor, Frank Redman. Although he has passed from this life, way before his time, his lessons in editing and writing live on.

More thanks to my friend and an amazing Author, Robin Barefield. Your willingness to read the roughest of drafts, and encourage me, helped this book come into being.

Further thanks to Wikipedia. It has become an excellent source for supernatural questions.

Gods and Monsters.com, https://www.gods-and-monsters.com/fairies-fae.html, and Listverse.com for fantastic articles on Fairies.

Andalusia Forest

The Theme Park for Millie seemed like the answer to fervent prayer. Lucius seemed like the savior Roy prayed for. Then, it all went wrong . . . So wrong!

On a rare occasion when Roy Torrens had a homecare nurse for his beloved child, he walked into a forest to be alone and to clear his mind. He had been trying to find a place he and his daughter could call home, where Millie would be free from ridicule, being spat upon, and called a freak because of her handicap.

Tears welled up in his eyes as he remembered all the pain his child had suffered at the hands of ignorant adults and children. His heart filled with hatred, reflecting on the most recent time—his final straw.

Roy left Millie outside the grocery store, eyes dancing with delight on the mechanical rocking horse.

"I'll be right back."

"It's okay, Daddy. I love riding!" Millie slapped the reigns against the iron horse's neck. "Giddy up!"

Roy smiled at seeing his sweet child so content. He walked into the store for milk and eggs.

At the checkout, a wail of despair pummeled his ears.

Millie!

He ran for the door, abandoning his possessions.

Millie lay helpless on the ground, her nose bleeding and two thin gashes above her right eye.

Two adolescent boys sniggered at her.

One sat atop Millie's prized mechanical horse. "Whatcha going to do about it, crybaby?"

Roy cleared the sidewalk in one giant step, collared the boy, and yanked him from the horse. "How dare you!"

The boy spat on Roy. "Whatcha going to do about it, Old Man?"

Roy's right hand shot skyward.

The boy cringed and ducked.

Roy dropped the boy to the ground.

"You are a child of the Devil! I hope you find out how it feels to be like Millie someday."

The other boy said, "Oh, that's telling him. Ha."

Roy gripped the boy by his shirt and raised his hand again. "You nasty, good-for-nothing. . ."

An unseen hand stopped his in midair. "That's enough, Sir."

Roy turned and stood face-to-face with a police officer.

He motioned at the two boys running away from the scene. "Those, those—ruffians attacked my daughter and threw her to the ground. They deserve a thrashing!"

The officer looked at Millie, her nose running red, scratches on her pale, pink skin where it had met the sidewalk. He shook his head.

"You best pick up your little one and clean her up." He turned and walked off.

Roy rushed to Millie. "I'm so sorry, Pumpkin. I should have never left you alone."

Millie sniffed. "No, Daddy. It was worth it. I got to be free and ride for just a minute. Like a real kid."

Roy felt the knife of despair go through his heart. "I promise you, Millie, someday you will walk, and no one, but no one, will ever be able to harm you again."

I will find us a place you can be free, Millie, I swear it!

Roy inquired around Wisteria about land for sale. Old Mr. Higgins, the proud proprietor of the only Café in town, said he might know a place. He yanked out an old map and pointed to acreage west of the city.

"And, this might be it," Roy said.

Roy walked the woodlands above a fantastic waterfall. He pushed his way through the almost impenetrable trees and shrubs surrounding the boulders of the cascading waters.

He trudged forward, the foliage unrelenting. "I may as well turn around before I can't find my way out," Roy said, breathing fast and shallow from fighting the dense vegetation. He glimpsed a shiny, dark blue color. He squinted and made his way to a line of trees, looking like stoic guards reaching for the cloudless blue sky.

He shimmied between two rough, brown trunks and stepped into a clearing. A round, aqua-blue pool of water shimmered in the afternoon sun. Roy strode to the pond. His reflection was perfectly clear, like the water. The puddle appeared bottomless. The aqua-blue turned to black several feet below. He caught hold of an eight-foot tree limb and stuck it into the water. It never touched bottom. He released it. The stick was sucked into the depths.

Roy shook his head in wonder.

"That pond is an enigma."

Roy jumped backward.

"Who are you?" Roy asked.

"My name is Lucius. Who are *you*? And why are you on my land?"

Roy studied Lucius. Something about him sent uncontrollable shivers up his spine. Roy couldn't put a finger on why this man frightened him. He'd fought in the Korean War and never felt this deep fear.

Lucius wore a tanned leather duster with coffee-colored buttons. It hit Lucius midcalf. The coat hung on the man's frame like an oversized quilt on its rack. Below the duster, Roy made out a pair of clean but worn blue jeans and shiny, black cowboy boots.

What's wrong with his eyes? Roy thought. *They are as dark as the cowboy boots yet shine like iridescent black pearls.*

Roy shook himself. "I apologize for intruding. I am looking to buy land. Someone said this acreage might be for sale."

Lucius's eyes twinkled with interest. "Really? Who would have told you such a thing?"

"An older man named Higgins. Then someone at the Pinkerly Farm mentioned it on my way out here."

"Mabel told you, did she? Why? What makes you so special as to mention this land?"

"I don't know. I explained my situation to the woman. I have a daughter who is in a wheelchair. I'm trying to find a place where we can live, and she can have freedom from being bullied. That's when Mabel told me about this place."

Lucius's eyebrows went up. "A daughter, you say?"

Roy nodded.

"My family has had this land for generations. I thought it may be time to let another have it. But I haven't found the right buyer—yet."

"I don't understand."

"I'm particular. Your reason for buying appeals to me. Meet me back here tonight. If you are serious."

"I am serious. I'll be here." Roy turned to leave.

"Wait!"

Roy turned, looked into the ebony eyes again, and shivered. "Yes?"

First, you must return to Pinkerly Farm. Tell Mabel Lucius sent you. She will give you a package. Bring it with you."

"I need to get back and tend to my daughter."

"That's your problem. But, if you are serious, you will do as I instruct. And bring your daughter with you tonight."

"Her wheelchair won't travel through all this." Roy waved his arm to the right and left, indicating the underbrush and ivy-covered trees beyond the small, open field.

"Bring her! You will find a way."

Roy shook his head. "Not happening. She does not need to be stranded in the middle of nowhere!"

"Mr. Torrens, I am aware of your hopes for your daughter. You want her to walk again."

"How do you know my name? More, how do you know my wishes for Millie? I've NEVER shared my dream with anyone!"

Lucius held up a hand. "Any loving parent would want their child to be normal. Do you want your daughter to walk again?"

"Of course I do."

"Bring her here tonight. As they say, where there is a will, there is a way. If you don't show up with your daughter, I'll assume you aren't serious. I will withdraw my offer to sell at midnight."

Terror seized Roy, and hope replaced it. *Why do I believe this man?*

"Because I'm telling you the truth. That's why you believe me."

Shock traveled at light speed up Roy's spine.

"No, I can't read your thoughts. But, I can assume them. I was right?"

"Yes."

"Then do as I instructed, and return here after sunset when the moon rises."

"I will try my best," Roy said over his shoulder as he exited the woods.

Roy pulled up to the Pinkerly farmhouse.

Mabel stood on her covered, whitewashed porch holding a small package wrapped in brown paper and secured with twine.

"Lucius sent me to talk to you."

Mabel held the bundle out further. "Take this with you tonight."

Roy took the bundle from Mabel. "How did you know?"

Mabel ignored the question. "Mr. Torrens, Lucius has been waiting for you for a long time. Don't cross him. Good luck." Mabel turned, walked through the screen door, and disappeared into the darkness of the house.

"Where are we going, Daddy?" Millie asked.

"To meet a new friend, someone with some land I want to buy."

"Oh," Millie said, disappointed.

"He is a nice man, Millie. If he will sell me this land, we will have a place for you to play—just for you."

"I guess."

Roy wheeled Millie to the top of the waterfall.

Millie looked at it. "That's a long way down."

"It is. But I've got you."

Roy guided the wheelchair toward the woods.

"Daddy, I won't fit in there! I'm scared."

"Well, let's go a little further. We'll go home if the vegetation is too dense for your chair. Okay?"

"Okay." Millie relaxed back into her chair.

Roy wheeled her to the edge of the timberland. He peered into the darkness. It was as before—overgrown with thick bushes and trees. His heart sank. He turned the wheelchair to head back to the car.

"Wait! There's a path." Millie directed Roy's attention to her left.

Roy squinted into the darkness. He spotted a skinny dirt walkway, barely big enough to fit a little girl's wheelchair. "This trail wasn't here earlier today."

He turned Millie toward the path. It headed directly to the glade.

The small pool of water glowed.

"Oh, that's beautiful. Push me over. I want to look closer."

Roy hesitated. He feared he'd strike a rock or dirt hump and send his precious child into the pool's depths.

"Come on, Daddy!"

Roy took a deep breath and started forward.

"I can see myself like it's a mirror! What is that beautiful light?"

"Good evening. I'm glad you could make it."

Roy whirled to face Lucius. "Where did you come from?"

"I've been here all along. I began to wonder if you'd chickened out."

"I said I'd be here if I could."

Lucius nodded and turned to the child. "You must be Millie." Lucius held out a sun-browned hand. The small child took it in her pale one.

"How do you do," Millie said.

Lucius smiled—a smile which did not go to his eyes. "And polite, too." He turned to Roy. "Do you have the package?"

Roy searched his shirt pockets and produced the small, brown box. "Here."

"Good. Give it to Millie."

Roy shot a questioning look at Lucius.

"Give it to Millie!"

Lucius faced Millie again. "Open it, Millie. It is a present for you—and for this land."

"A present? For me?" Millie tore into the small package and pulled out a glass pendant on a shiny, gold chain. She stared at it.

"What do you think?"

"Oh, it is beautiful. I've never seen anything so pretty."

"It is magical. So magical only special people can touch it."

"Really?"

"Yes. And, because your father is special, he can touch it, too. Do you want to wear it?"

"Oh, YES!"

"Roy, would you put it on her?"

"I think you should. After all, you gave it to Millie."

"NO!" Lucius cleared his throat. "No. I would like you to do it."

Roy put the pendant on Millie. It was a perfect fit and length. "What do you say, Millie?"

Millie dropped her head to her chest and said, "Thank you."

"You are most welcome."

"Now, Roy, from what I understand, you want a place for Millie to play. Am I right?"

"Yes."

"This is your place if you still want it."

"How much?"

"Oh, the price isn't money."

"I thought this was too good to be true. Come on, Millie." Roy reached for the amulet to return it to Lucius.

"Hear me out. It's the least you can do."

Roy turned back to Lucius. "I'm listening."

"This land is yours. But I request you build a fantasy village, an enchanted village, and open it to the public upon completion. You will make money from it; Millie will have what she has wanted, which is her own playground – acres and acres of it."

"I wanted a place for Millie where she won't be ridiculed."

"I understand. And who will ridicule the daughter of the owner of a fantasy park? Who, that is, who wants to be able to come and play here? You have the right to kick anyone who does so off the property. Millie can make friends. She will be important. When you see these changes, we can talk about her walking."

"Walking?" Millie echoed.

"Yes. The amulet I gave you is magical."

"How does it work?"

"Well, first, you wear it until you are a young woman. When you turn sixteen, it must be placed, levitated, over this pool forever. As long as it stays there, you will be changed. You, Millie, will own this place and will be strong and powerful. What do you say?"

"Quit telling my daughter such fibs."

"I am not lying, sir. Millie, how do you feel right now?"

"Ok."

"Move your legs."

"Stop it! You are more cruel than all the adults and children who've tormented her combined."

Lucius turned black, angry eyes on Roy. "Silence!" He smiled at Millie and gently said, "Now, move your legs."

Millie looked at and concentrated on her toes, willing them to move. She slumped back into her chair. "Nothing."

"Try again."

Millie groaned in an effort to move. Her leg twitched. She smiled.

Roy's eyes widened as his daughter moved both legs. She tried to push herself out of the chair and fell to the ground.

"She won't be able to stand on her own. Not yet. She will be able to use canes, though." Lucius produced two Diamond Willow matching canes. "Try these."

Millie put one in each hand and pulled herself up. She wobbled, leaned more on the canes, and stood.

"As long as Millie wears the pendant, she will have limited use of her legs."

"It's a miracle. Thank you, Lucius."

Lucius held up his hand. "Don't thank me. When the time is right, I will come to you. When I appear, the pendant must be suspended over the pool to never be touched again. Millie, as I said, you will be changed and have all the power and strength you'd ever want. Sound good?"

"Yes!" Millie's eyes narrowed. She smiled, thinking of being more potent than those who made fun of her.

"Do you agree, Roy? Do you agree to build the attractions and, when I say, to suspend this amulet over the pool?"

"Yes."

"So be it. It is done."

———————————

Roy Torrens gripped the mahogany-stained railing of the porch of his new home. He smiled as he surveyed the buildings and rides beyond.

Millie stood beside him, Diamond Willow canes supporting her thin frame.

"What do you think, Millie? Are you going to love living here?" He looked down at the golden-haired child who had just turned sixteen.

Millie Torrens looked up at her father. "Oh, I hope so. Did you put up a fairy statue like I asked?

"Of course," Jeremia answered.

Millie smiled at her father.

"I know it's been hard for you to wait and see the park. But I couldn't risk you being injured while it was being built. We lost five workers on the Haunted House exhibit alone."

"I understand, Daddy."

"Before you ask, I created Andalusia Forest from your favorite nursery rhymes." He drew Millie's attention to her left. "Over there are Jack and Jill and a real working well."

Millie squinted. Her eyes brightened with delight. "Oh, I see them!"

Roy turned. "And over there is the old bad witch's house from Hansel and Gretel and Little Miss Muffet's Spider House and, for fun, the haunted house I spoke of."

Millie leaned forward on her canes, straining to lay eyes on the attractions. "When can I go?"

Roy held his daughter's petite hands and said, "In a few minutes."

I do wish you could really walk, Pumpkin. Roy thought.

"Really?"

"Yes. And I've made sure you can go anywhere you want here." Roy motioned at the slightly sloping ramps zigzagging through the twenty-five-acre tract.

Millie caressed the blue glass necklace around her neck. "Will it be safe here?"

Roy looked at Millie, puzzled. "Why do you ask about it being safe?"

Millie studied her black patent leather shoes. "Because it's special. If a mean person gets it, it would be bad."

"Sweetie, you remember what Lucius said, right?"

"Yes," Millie mumbled.

"Andalusia Forest is complete. Soon the pendant must be placed over the pool in the center of this place." Roy studied the sky-blue glass, sparkling as it caught a ray of sunshine. Inside was a mahogany-colored inch-long thorn.

Millie fingered the glass, gripping the pendant in a tight fist.

"You can go look at it anytime."

"Promise."

"Promise."

"Okay."

"It will look beautiful over the aquamarine-colored water. See how this glass is almost the same color?"

Millie nodded.

No one can take it once it is suspended over the water."

"Ok. Know what?"

"What?"

"I think this pendant has magic—protection magic. It will keep us safe from bad people. I KNOW it."

Roy smiled at his daughter, who believed in fairies, good witches, and unicorns. She would have believed in God if he'd allowed it.

If there were a God! How could He let this happen to such an innocent, happy child? The way Roy felt about God, this amulet was more likely to protect them.

"I'm sure it will, sweetheart."

———

Roy surveyed the opening day crowd. Red, blue, and yellow balloons floated above the heads of the mass.

I didn't think this day would ever come. So many tragedies occurred before I could even open the gates.

Joe, the construction helper he'd hired, was the first. He was using a pulley and rope to haul the eight-foot black spider (more like a tarantula) onto the top of the Miss Muffet exhibit. It broke. Somehow the statue landed on top of Joe, squashing him like a human bug.

Later, a young woman named Sue from the mental asylum near Hayden snuck in and climbed to the top of the haunted house. Jagged rocks surrounded the house awaiting installation. Sue took a swan dive off the highest turret and landed square on a knife-sharp point, impaling her small frame.

The list went on and on. Roy recalled the shattered windows, mysterious malfunctions of forklifts and excavators, and frays in ropes and cables. Almost every malfunction led to broken bones, concussions, and even one decapitation.

Roy shook his head and came out of the memories. Foreboding tugged at his gut as it had during the construction. *Just accidents, that's all!*

"Welcome," Roy shouted.

The crowd continued in excited noise.

He clutched a megaphone. "WELCOME!"

The crowd quieted to a few whispers; A crying child protesting his or her hunger rose to Roy on the stage. A red-haired mom bounced the toddler up and down in her arms, released a bottle from an oversized bag, and stuck it in the baby's mouth.

"Today is a day I never thought would happen. I am opening Andalusia Forest. I built this for my daughter Millie." He put his hand on his daughter's thin shoulder. "But, as Millie told me, we must share it with the world. And, so I am."

The crowd cheered.

"So, why isn't it free, Mr. Torrens?" An overall-clad youth shouted from the middle of the throng.

"Well, I do need to eat, Jeffrey. And, I must keep the popcorn coming you all like so much."

Laughter issued from the gathering.

"If you put it like that," Jeffrey said.

"Are you ready for fairytales to come to life?"

"YES."

"Are you ready to have your children play in a safe environment without fear of being bullied?"

"YES."

Roy cut the red ribbon with the ornamental scissors he borrowed from Wisteria's Mayor. "Come on in!"

The throng made their way into Andalusia Forest, two at a time, moms holding children's hands, young loves holding each other's.

Roy smiled when the throng broke into smaller groups and scattered into different parts of the acreage.

Roy descended the steps to an asphalt walkway. The path split in two directions. One sign pointed left, *Witch's House, Spider Domain*; the second sign pointed to the right, *Lover's Lane, Jack and Jill, and Fairy Land*.

Roy's eyes narrowed when he saw two boys, Johnny Elder and Timmy Delworth, the bullies who threw Millie off the mechanical horse.

They raced after Millie toward the Witch House.

Good for nothings. How did you get in here?

Roy started after them.

"They won't hurt your girl again," Roy whirled and faced Lucius.

"Lucius! I haven't seen you since we agreed on the land. How did you find out about those boys?"

"I know many things." Lucius's eyes turned ink-black, then cleared as speedily as they had turned. "It's a small town. Word gets around." He smiled.

Roy studied Lucius. "I suppose."

"You have not completed our bargain."

"I've built the park."

"You have not completed our bargain," Lucius said. "She still wears the necklace."

Roy's shoulders slumped. "She loves it so much."

"Both of you knew this day would come."

Roy exhaled. "Yes."

"It must be done tonight. Otherwise, Millie will lose all use of her legs again. Do you want that?"

"No!"

"I'll see you tonight."

"Yes. First, I must see about those boys, Lucius."

Lucius smirked. "They've already been dealt with."

Roy spun around at the sound of screams—not of joy but of terror. He turned back. Lucius was gone. He scanned the grounds in all directions. Lucius had vanished.

A chill ran up Roy's spine. He knew something wasn't right about Lucius. He always felt uncomfortable, no terrified, when the man was near. Like prey sensing the predator was close and it was about to be devoured.

Roy shook himself free and ran up the walk toward the Witch House. Millie stood over two boys, laughing down at them.

"Millie! What have you done?"

"Nothing."

"What happened?"

"Well, they started laughing at me and throwing stones. Called me a freaky cripple. So, the witch took care of them." Millie smiled up at her dad. The look in her eyes sent a second chill through him.

"What do you mean?"

"Something green came out of the witch's eyes, right at them." Millie grinned. "They fell to the ground and started crying. Like the big crybabies they are!" She shouted.

"That's not true!" The oldest boy, Johnny, said. "She threw something hot on us, and we are scalded. Look!"

Roy looked down at the boys. Red welts popped up on their hands and shorts-clad legs. Angry, red blisters replaced the bumps, and puss seeped out of each sore.

Roy called out to the gathering crowd. "Is there a doctor here somewhere? Anyone with medical training? These boys are really hurt."

"I'm a nurse." An older woman with straight grey hair came forward.

Roy stepped to the side.

"I'm Mrs. Farns. What do we have here?"

By this time, the boys were whimpering from the pain.

Mrs. Farns bent over and took in the sores. "These aren't from hot water. These look to be an infection—if I didn't know better, I'd say it's smallpox."

A suntanned man in bib overalls stared at Mrs. Farns and, hearing the word, screamed, "Everyone out! Now! Grab your kids."

"I'll call an ambulance." Roy turned and ran toward the 'Fairyland' sign to the walkway and took a right at Jack and Jill's statues—he almost fell over Jack's prostrate body at the bottom of the hill where the well stood. He ran the short dirt trail to the office, flung open the door, and stepped inside. He snatched the telephone from its base.

"Tonight!" Lucius said.

Roy dropped the phone from the shock of hearing the voice coming from nowhere, yet all around him. *My nerves are playing tricks on me.*

He picked up the telephone and punched Zero.

"Operator."

"This is Roy Torrens at Andalusia Forest. Send an ambulance quickly."

"Yes, sir."

Roy waved to the two men in white coats to follow him.

When the men saw the oozing sores on the boys' hands and legs, they gloved their hands. "Call Dr. Daniels, tell him we have possible smallpox, and to prepare a quarantine room." They turned to Roy. "You must close now. It is under quarantine until we pin down the boys' disease."

"Are such extreme measures essential? We are in the fresh air. These boys didn't even enter one of the amusement buildings, did they Millie?"

"No. Timmy and Johnny chased me until the witch sent the green stuff out of her eyes."

"Green stuff?"

"I haven't a clue what she's talking about. It's a child's imagination. Right, Millie?"

Millie pursed her lips and glared at her father.

"What has gotten into you, young lady?"

"Nothing, Daddy. I'm just fine. I saw green stuff. Why don't *you* believe me?"

"Anyway, I'll talk to you later." Roy turned to the ambulance attendants. "As you can tell, they haven't been anywhere."

"Smallpox is nothing to sneeze at, Mr. Torrens," Jeffrey, the blond, taller of the two attendants, remarked.

"If it's not smallpox, you can reopen. You are closed until we are sure this disease is not contagious."

Roy trudged back to the office. He flicked the switch entitled 'Megaphones' to activate the prominent speakers atop poles throughout Andalusia Forest.

"Ladies and Gentlemen, I'm sorry, but we must close until further notice. Please make your way to the front gates as quickly as possible."

Many people grumbled as they made their way to the front.

"We paid good money to see this place," Mrs. Goodall told Roy.

"When we reopen, it's free," Roy answered.

Mrs. Goodall glared at him.

"You can have a free ice cream—for you and your kids."

Alright. "Let's go," Mrs. Goodall said as she led her brood to the gates.

Roy lifted the handheld megaphone. "And the same goes for the rest of you, too."

The grumbling quieted.

Mike Troopy, Roy Torrens' only friend in the area, stopped. "Sorry for the mess this must have put you in, Roy."

"Thanks, Mike."

———

Roy wandered the deserted park. Millie walked beside him, slowly placing one leg before the other.

"Millie, we must put your necklace above the pond tonight."

"Okay."

Roy looked at her with surprise. "You're not upset?"

"No."

"Why?"

"Because I want to be strong, stronger than anyone else, so no one can ever make fun of me again. Lucius said I would be once we put the stone above the pool."

"I'm not sure Lucius was telling the truth."

"Oh, yes, he was. An angel told me."

"An angel?"

"Well, it looked like an angel. It told me right before those boys tried to attack me, and the green stuff shot from the witch's eyes. It told me we had to put the glass amulet over the pool, and then I'd be changed forever."

"I love you the way you are, Millie."

Millie smiled, the first tender smile her dad had seen in a long time. In fact, since she had started wearing the amulet. "I know. And I will always remember it. You have my word. I love you, too, Daddy."

"I did tell Lucius we would do this. And I always keep my word."

"I am going to change, Daddy. The angel told me. I'm going to become someone different. Please don't be scared. As long as you are alive, I will never do anything to hurt you."

Roy looked at his daughter, sadness in his eyes. "I know you would never hurt me, Pumpkin. Why would you say something like that?"

"You'll understand soon."

At dusk, Roy and Millie strolled to the small meadow. Dark blanketed the dale before they arrived.

It was a moonless night. Roy could not find his hand in front of his face. They would have been entirely in the dark without the old lantern he'd brought.

The pool glowed a blood-red light.

A dark, hooded figure stood beside the water.

"Hello?" Roy said.

The man turned.

"Lucius?"

"Some call me Lucius. But Millie knows my real name, don't you, Millie?"

Millie smiled. "Yes."

"Who do you say I am?"

"You are my Master and the only one who will help me."

"And who else do you say I am?"

"Some call you the Devil."

"You are correct."

Roy looked at Lucius, "What's going on here?"

"Millie and I have talked many times since the first day you brought her here. We talk in her dreams. She has agreed to follow the plan I've laid out for her to live—a design for a warrior, not a victim. The process where she will bring destruction on all she deems should be destroyed."

Roy turned to Millie. "Millie, what is he talking about?"

"He has come to me in my dreams. But I was asked not to tell you. So, I didn't. Besides, I'm old enough to make my own decisions. I want to be what he says I can be."

Terror struck Roy like a bolt of lightning. He clutched Millie's hand. "No, Millie, we are leaving!" He yanked at her to move.

Millie remained still. "I am staying." Millie tucked one cane under her arm and released the chain with her free hand. She held it out to Lucius.

The black eyes turned as red as the pond. Lucius smiled, baring sharp, jagged teeth. An ochre-green liquid dripped from the fangs. "I can't touch the amulet. It is of the Holy One. You must hang it over the pond as you agreed."

Millie held it out to her dad. "You must do this."

"How?" Roy asked.

Lucius waved his hand. Large sticks danced into view. He pointed. The bars floated over to the pool and hovered above it. They arranged themselves in a triangle, with the straightest of the rods levitating above the pond toward Roy.

It reminded Roy of the bones of a teepee.

"Loop the chain around the small stick in the middle."

Roy walked to the pool and placed the chain onto the stick. The branch moved into the center of the tripod, making it impossible to be retrieved from the pool's edge.

"It is now done," Lucius said.

"I don't feel so good!" Millie wailed.

The sound sent knives of despair into Roy's soul. This noise came from Millie's innermost being.

Roy ran toward his beloved daughter just as a dark cloud enveloped her. An invisible force sent him flying backward to the edge of the forest.

He landed with an "Oomph!" He shook himself and took off toward the dark cloud again.

"Stand!" Lucius commanded.

Roy stopped in midstride, willing himself to move but unable to.

A low, threatening laugh came from Lucius. "The transformation will be completed. This is what you both agreed to; this is what will happen."

The screams from Millie started to subside and were replaced with a sharp clicking sound. The clicking grew louder. The smokey vapor cleared.

Instead of trying to run forward, Roy willed himself to retreat. He still couldn't move.

"Daddy." A clicking sound followed the words.

Roy's eyes grew wide. "Millie?"

"I was known as Millie. From this day forward, you will call me Mildred."

"What have you done with my child?" Roy looked at Lucius.

"Your child is now your guardian. And, the guardian of this enchanted place."

"No! I did not agree to this!"

"You did, Roy Torrens. More importantly, your daughter did. Can't you see? She will no longer be bullied. She is no longer crippled. She is a warrior."

Roy Torrens looked at the creature standing not fifteen feet from him. He felt repulsed. He shuddered. *Stop it! Look at her!*

Roy took in the abomination before him. This Mildred was jet black, with long, spikey thorns of fur covering her legs and abdomen. And her legs? She had eight of them. She towered over him—at least twenty feet tall. But the scariest horror was the fangs. They protruded from each side of the jet-black, moist mouth. They click-clacked when she spoke.

"It is me, Daddy."

Roy looked into the iridescent blue eyes of this Mildred. He saw his child there—only briefly. But it was enough to make him care about, if not love, this creature. He nodded.

"From this day forward, no one will harm me. Or you. I am your protector. And I will live on long after you. Once you die, I will make this place mine and mine alone. Until then, it is yours. People will come. Sometimes, though, I must eat. So, some people will have to die."

"No, Mildred! I'll bring you food."

Mildred's mouth creaked when she laughed. "You can't feed me enough. But you can try."

"I'll bring in some sheep and cows."

"It's a start. I'll try not to eat the people. But I won't promise."

A tear traced its way down Roy's sun-red cheek. "Please . . . "

"Go," Mildred commanded.

"Where will you be?"

"Around. I'll find you sometimes. I will always be close to Lucius and the pond. When you see him, you will realize I am near."

Roy strode back toward the amusement park's main pathway. Dense brush and grass grew behind him until the trail to the glade disappeared behind him.

CHAPTER 1

Kat leaped from behind the cabinet in the boat's galley. *And this is where the rubber leaves the steel belted radial,* she thought. Kat raised her arms, brandishing a cast iron skillet like a Samurai sword.

A man, Charlie Fargus by name, had been in a great conversation with her just a few moments before. Then, like lightning streaks in a mini-second across the sky, Charlie changed.

And I mean changed! His face turned a sallow green; his eyes took on the color of tar—the whites as black as the pupils.

Kat dove behind the counter right before Charlie snatched her by the hair.

Ken ran into the small living area of the boat. "What the h…" Ken stopped in his tracks.

The new Charlie spun and faced Ken.

Ken's eyes widened. Charlie's hands had become green, scaly, five-fingered paws with the longest nails Ken had ever seen.

Charlie lunged forward, nicking the side of Ken's shirt. A minute rivulet of blood seeped onto the white, red, and black cloth.

"Ouch!" Ken yelled and clutched his side.

Kat slammed the skillet into Charlie's left ear.

Charlie snarled, swung his arms back and forth in the air trying to locate Kat, stopped, tumbled to his knees, and fell face forward onto the teak floorboards.

"Who or *what* is that?" Kat asked.

"Well," Ken replied, "the closest thing I've read about is a Parlangua—a Louisiana legend."

Kat glanced down at the inanimate green monster on the floor and up at Ken. "And what is a Parlangua?"

"It's a legend of a half man, half crocodile."

Kat bent forward and perused the man's features. Charlie's sun-bathed face with a dash of freckles on the cheeks and nose was now olive-green and iridescent. Kat poked the skin with a finger. "Yep. He has scales."

"What do we have here? Some kind of southern monster?"

"Being I don't believe in monsters—at least not this kind of monster—I'd say we are dealing with more demons," Ken said.

"So, any plan?"

"Tie him up. We'll call for backup."

"Backup?"

"Yep. You call Bart. I'll call Pastor Lucas in Ravens Cove," Ken said.

Kat nodded and dialed.

Ken went to the forward bay in the boat and pulled out a blue, heavy rope. "This should work." He set about tying the man-creature's hands and feet.

"You want me to exercise a demon from 4,000 miles away? Over the phone?" Paul Lucas asked.

"Unless you have a better idea."

"How about the preacher who lives by your Aunt Rose? Pastor Morton? Can't he come?"

"Nope. He is at a conference and won't return until next week."

Lucas sighed. "I'm not sure this will work. But, put the phone to the man's ear."

"Bart will be here in 30 minutes," Kat interrupted.

Ken nodded, knelt, and put the mobile to the bloody ear, courtesy of Kat's goodnight kiss with a skillet.

"DEMON," Paul shouted through the phone. "In the name of Jesus, who are you?"

The man responded with a low growl, stirred, and strained against the ropes binding his hands.

"It's working, Pastor," Ken said, returning the phone to the man's ear.

"Demon. Your name!" Paul Lucas shouted.

"I am many," the growling voice said.

"Give me all of your names!"

Charlie uttered a string of curses, followed by a string of names.

Kat caught Tomak and Robith out of what seemed like a hundred.

Paul rebuked each by name in the name of Jesus.

"How does he remember all those names?" Kat asked Ken.

Ken put a finger to his mouth to silence her.

"The Holy Spirit reminds me of those names," Paul said. "Now pray with me."

"In the mighty name of Jesus, be gone each and every spirit I have named here. Leave and do not return. As the Lord ordains, it is done!" Paul shouted.

"Now move as far back as you can," Paul said.

Ken and Kat raced up the narrow steps to the top deck and ran starboard. The boat vibrated and groaned against its moorings. The water around them churned up into violent waves.

Kat held fast to the railing with one hand and Ken with the other.

A black cloud billowed up the galley steps. Shrieks issued from the fog, forcing Ken and Kat to let go of the railing and cover their ears. The mist shot skyward, hovered, and dove into the water 50 feet from the boat.

A moan came from below.

"Charlie!" Kat and Ken ran back down.

Charlie Fargus sat on the floor, hand over his ear, eyes dazed. "What in the name of all that's good happened?" He mumbled.

"Well, funny thing . . . " Kat said.

"Hello?" Bart's baritone drifted to them below deck.

"Here."

Bart lumbered down the steps and stopped midway to scrutinize the chaotic scene.

A man with a bloody ear sat dazed in the middle of the floor, Kat holding a kitchen towel against it. Ken was on the phone, asking for medical assistance.

"Do I need to ask?"

"No," Ken and Kat answered in unison.

I am assuming this gentleman was not who he seemed?" Bart asked.

"Not at all. But he's good now."

"Pastor Lucas says hello."

Bart raised an eyebrow. "That's all I need to know for now."

Kat turned to Ken. "Can we go home to Ravens Cove now? I've had about all the fun I can stand on this trip. I need a vacation from our vacation."

CHAPTER 2

Kat Tovslosky-Melbourne dropped her head into her hands, took a deep breath, then looked up. "So let me get this straight. You are just now informing me you have a sister named Chloe, who is not your sister but your cousin and is also the estranged daughter of Aunt Rose."

"Right," Ken Melbourne said.

"Why didn't I hear about her earlier?"

Ken sighed. "She and Aunt Rose have not been on the best of terms. And, to be honest, with all the battles we've fought in the past few months, it simply slipped my mind."

"And, this Chloe is a paranormal investigator."

"Right again."

"And she wants your help, our help here in East Texas?"

"That's what the message said."

"Are you crazy?"

"Not the last time I checked."

"And you're considering it?"

Ken narrowed his eyes, the color on his face rising. "She's my family, Kat. Of course, I'm considering it."

Kat's emerald green eyes met Ken's stormy blue ones. "You realize we came back here to visit your aunt and immediately return to Ravens Cove. You remember our agreement, right?"

"Last time I checked, my memory was still ok."

"Why is this so important to you? I thought we were avoiding the supernatural—real or imagined for a while. You realize I'm still recovering from my near death—real death—experience in the swamps here in East Texas."

"Yes. But we also agreed to help anyone in trouble like we had. And it sounds like Chloe may be getting herself into such a situation. She's young, Kat. She doesn't understand what she is dealing with. She thinks all the ghosty things are lost souls. And some probably are. But you and I often recognize those lost souls aren't lost at all—they are trying to take yours, mine, or anyone they can fool."

"You're right. We did agree to help others whenever needed. When do we leave?" Kat asked.

"When does who leave?" Bart asked, walking into the kitchen at Aunt Rose's house.

"We're going up to a place called Torrens Falls," Ken said.

"Why?" Bart asked.

"Seems Ken has a, well, sister—cousin who may be getting herself in trouble in the supernatural sense."

"This can't be happening," Bart said. "We are supposed to be back in the Cove tomorrow."

"No one is stopping you from going back," Ken said. "As for me, I'm going to help my cousin."

"And I'm not letting him go alone," Kat said.

Bart looked at the determination in his cousin's eyes. He looked at the stubbornness in Ken's.

"Well, you aren't doing this by yourselves. You two find trouble no matter where you end up."

"It follows us," Ken said.

"I'm canceling my trip back. Kat, you call Grandma Bricken and explain." Bart put the cell phone to his ear, turned on his heel, and disappeared into the dark narrow hallway off the kitchen.

"And, so, another adventure begins," Kat murmured.

CHAPTER 3

Andalusia Forest

The day came up blue-skyed and bright as it should on a spring day in East Texas. Chloe Melbourne breathed in the honey aroma of Blackfoot daisies and the light fragrance of Anacacho orchids, all laced with the scent of purple wisterias. "Great day to be alive!" She breathed.

The shrill ring of a phone shattered her peace.

Chloe took another breath of the spring aromas. "Hello?"

"He's missing! He might be dead."

"Jet?" Chloe closed her eyes. Jethro Cates, the bane of her existence. Correction. The blight of the entire town of Wisteria.

"Yeah, it's me. Listen up. Shank is missing."

Shank Groober, another stain on the town. "Shank goes missing a bunch, Jet. He always turns up."

"Not this time!" Jet shouted.

Chloe pulled the phone away from her ear and snarled, "If you'd like to continue this conversation, don't yell."

"Sorry," Jet muttered.

The apology reminded Chloe of a child, held by his ear and forced to say the words. *Not far from the truth where Jet is concerned,* Chloe thought.

A smooth, soft-spoken southern accent replaced the shout. "Shank has been gone for three days. He told me he was going to the old, abandoned amusement park by Torrens Falls. Said he needed extra cash and was going scavenging."

"So? Three days isn't long."

"He had a hot date with Sandra Cummins last evening. She called and, amidst the expletives about being stood up and what she thought of Shank's manhood, stated he hadn't shown up. Shank wouldn't miss a date with her. He's been trying to get Sandra to go out for months."

Chloe chewed the left corner of her mouth. "Hmmm."

"And there's something else."

"Listening," Chloe said.

"Well, he went looking for that thorn."

"What thorn?" Chloe played stupid.

"Don't play dumb. You know Andalusia Forest is rumored to be haunted by more than a silly ghost. It's rumored to be defended by— well—demons. And the thorn is supposed to be somewhere in there under some kind of hocus pocus."

"That's an old wives' tale."

"That all you can say?"

"Why do you need my help? Why not go up there by yourself and find the guy?"

"I'm not crazy! You've heard the same stories I have. People go in and never come out. And, as I said before, it's haunted."

"And you'd let a childish rumor stop you from finding your best friend?"

"You bet I would! Shank's my pal. I'm not dying for him!"

"Always so gallant, Jet."

"Come on, Chloe, if anyone can find him, you can. You've got a ghost-hunting gig, right? If you check it out and tell me it isn't haunted, I can come up and look for myself."

"If you're so worried, why haven't you called the police?"

"Right. And get Shank arrested for thieving? Shank would rather be dead. Friend or not, he'd kill me."

Chloe thought back to the elementary school days with Shank and Jet. If the truth be known, she had and still did avoid Shank and Jet at all costs. It didn't take much to send Shank into fight mode. He almost killed little Jimmy Fellows for running into him on the playground. Blacked both Jimmy's eyes, broke his rib, and sent him to the hospital. Shank got suspended for the rest of the school year. And a record with the juvenile courts.

"I see your point."

"It's not just missing the date, Chloe. Shank's mom is feeling poorly. He promised her he'd be back within 24 hours. You know how he loves his mama."

A jolt of alarm hit Chloe's heart. She sat up statue-straight. "Ok. You've got my attention. You paying?"

Silence answered her.

"Well?"

"I don't have much money."

"We can take it out in trade."

"Oh, I like your idea!" Jet laughed.

"Haha! Not funny, you creep! The ghostly van needs engine work. You fix it for free. I'll go to Torrens Falls. Deal?"

Again, silence. It was so thick Chloe felt like she could cut through it with a jigsaw blade.

"Fine," Jet growled. "When are you going?"

"I'll find Darci. We can leave in the morning."

"You better!" The phone went dead.

CHAPTER 4

P art of the human protocol, manners if you will, is to invite a person into our lives. To ask someone to become a friend, join a group, go out for lunch. Who doesn't comprehend this unspoken rule, for heaven's sake?" Chloe Melbourne screamed in her head.

"The answer? A conscious entity," Chloe said aloud.

"Who knew?" Chloe shook her head and muttered, "I know now."

Chloe thought back to her last paranormal investigation. She could still picture a black figure, a shadow figure, some said, running down the dark hallway of the abandoned warehouse.

I stood frozen, trying to catch the entity on film. When I realized it wasn't stopping, I dropped the camera, like a buffoon, and raced for the control room and the safety of my friends. I felt like a powerful electric jolt punched me in the back. The next thing I remember is coming around with Darci standing over her.

"Oh my gosh! Look at the left side of your face!" Darci remarked.

Chloe threw a hand up to her cheek. "Ouch." When she touched it, it burned.

For days afterward, Chloe felt malevolent eyes watching her every move. Her house, which had always been her safe haven, became a scene out of *Paranormal Encounters.* Drawers opened and closed on their own; lights flickered on and off, floorboards creaked under the weight of invisible boots.

"Yes, but I called Pastor Morton, and he took care of it," Chloe said.

He took care of the entity but couldn't heal your insides, A voice whispered into Chloe's mind.

Darci Ludholtz stuck her head into Cloe's room. "You ready?"

"Ready? Will I ever be ready?" Chloe whispered.

Darci glared at Chloe. "Well, I suppose that's a rhetorical question? If not, why is the van packed, and why am I waiting for you?"

Chloe squeezed her eyes tight. *Why this dread? It's another job. Come on, Chloe, shake it off!*

Chloe took a long breath and exhaled. She looked around her room. The one place she still felt safe. The cream-colored linen curtains floated up and down in the spring breeze, like an invisible hand raised and dropped them, only to catch them again before they touched the window frame. "I just need a minute."

Darci gripped Chloe's shoulders. "Look at me! Your cousin is going to meet us in three hours. We need to move if we are going to make it on time."

Kenneth Melbourne and his bride, Kat, were visiting Chloe's mom, Rose, a couple of towns over from Wisteria. Rose had beaten the odds against an aggressive brain cancer which stopped growing in a mysterious and perplexing fashion and went into complete remission.

Chloe sniggered at the memory of Kat and Ken having a 'shotgun' wedding at Mom's house so she could see her favorite, albeit only, nephew get married. Rose raised Ken like a son after his parents were killed. He was the only child until Rose received some fantastic news.

I was a surprise. Chloe thought.

The doctors told Rose Melbourne she couldn't ever have children. Lord knows she and her dad tried. Yet, here she was. A testament to the God Mom always went on and on about. The one Chloe wasn't sure existed but sure knew enough about.

"Oh, rats! I forgot. Coming!" Chloe snatched a gray and blue backpack from the foot of her bed.

An ink-black storm cloud shaped like a wraith materialized—long, gray sleeves flowed from both sides of the cloud, and a full-length ash-colored robe wafted around it. The enigma descended on the house like a dark wave onto a white sand beach.

Chloe dropped her bag and went to the window. *Where did that come from?* She caught hold of the lower sill to pull it shut, then stopped. A cool breeze, laced with the smell of ions, drifted into her nostrils right before a malevolent snarl reached her ears.

The shadow man is back! Terror filled her stomach.

Chloe drew in a ragged breath. She stood taller, setting her face like a stone toward the sniggering shape. "So it begins! So be it." She exclaimed.

Chloe slammed the window and jogged through the living room to the van.

CHAPTER 5

Chloe studied the wraith-shaped cloud from her shotgun position in the van. Relief flooded her as it faded from sight and didn't follow them out onto the highway.

"What's the matter with you?" Darci asked.

"Nothing," Chloe said.

"Not true," Darci answered.

"It's a bad feeling. I've had it since we said we'd go to Torrens Falls."

"You always have a sense of foreboding. On every paranormal investigation," Darci said.

"This one's different. I'm scared."

"Look. I understand you haven't been on an investigation since the warehouse episode. This is the perfect way to start again. It's an easy in and out. Talk to the park rangers. Look for Shank. A few EVPs to satisfy Jet that it isn't haunted, and we're gone," Darci said in her matter-of-fact and down-to-earth tone.

"You, Darci, are an enigma," Chloe said.

"Why? Because I'm logical and hunt ghosts?"

"Yeah."

"When one comes from a long line of 'soothsayers,' as they were called, expounding on all the spirits surrounding us, yet I never saw one of them prove they were communicating with the other side. Logic is the answer. Of course, one day . . ." Darci's voice trailed off.

"One day, you saw the white lady near White Rock Lake in Dallas."

"Yeah. I couldn't explain the entity or find it. I was sure we'd run right over the woman. Then, I found out others had seen the same thing.

I talked to a few of them. They reported the same experience. Still, it must be a prank."

"And you've been trying to prove the paranormal is just a hoax ever since," Chloe surmised.

"And I will. This may be the time." Darci said.

The drive to Torrens Falls was spectacular. The weather was cool enough to keep the windows cracked and warm enough to wear her most comfy t-shirt. Chloe caught the sound of chickadees twittering for a mate, mingling with the melodious song of Robins and sparrows. Chloe smiled. She relaxed a bit. *Darci is right. I'm being silly.*

Torrens Falls was more than beautiful. It was awe-inspiring. Glorious pink, pitted boulders confined a waterfall thundering over grey stepping stones and pooling in a small lake forty feet below. The water overflowed into a glistening stream to meander into more significant spillways miles from this tucked-away Texas location. A few hundred feet above stood Andalusia Forest. Cottages and treehouses of an abandoned theme park dotted the landscape.

More like a creepy, abandoned fairytale village straight out of someone's nightmares, Chloe thought.

Chloe strode up the pitted trail toward the park. She eyed a replica of an old oak tree, towering twenty feet in the air, with a witch's mouth as the door. Above the mouth was a hooked nose, complete with a wart, which acted as a roof. The *piece de resistance* was a triangular-shaped, black hat banded in green and white stripes. The eeriness factor increased to downright creepy in contrast to the beauty of the nearby falls. To the left of the witch tree stood statues of a small girl and boy. Both held gingerbread and red and white lollipops in their hands.

"Not a welcoming rendition of Hansel and Gretel," Chloe said.

To her immediate right, a small, once light blue cottage jutted up between an outcropping of sharp stones. Its dwarf-size door stood open as if inviting its next victim into their doom.

"Okay. This is creepy," Darci muttered.

"How sick does a person have to be to think up these horrible attractions?" Chloe asked.

"There are some scary stories about this place."

"Yeah. I suppose you need to tell me one, Ms. Historian?"

Darci smiled. "Always thought history is a strong foundation when hunting ghosts."

"Get on with it—wait!" Chloe waved in the direction of two men and a woman. "There's Ken and Kat!"

"Who is the third person?" Darci asked.

Chloe squinted in their direction. "No idea." She jogged toward the trio.

Ken opened his arms, and Chloe fell into them.

"How are you, Pip Squeak?" He mumbled into her thick, red hair.

"Better now because you're here!" Chloe held on tight. The foreboding she'd felt evaporated. Ken was her hero. She was safe when with him. She let go and pointed with her chin toward the second man. "Who's this?"

A tall, stocky man stepped forward and extended his hand. "I'm Bart Andersen. Cousin to this crazy, raven-haired woman."

Chloe shook his hand and said, "What brings you here?"

"I've learned to not let these two go anywhere without me. Especially if the words haunted, possessed, or murder are in the same sentence." Bart smiled.

Chloe shot Bart a questioning glance. "I understand, I think."

Darci joined Chloe. "This is my friend. And fellow paranormal investigator." Chloe made introductions all around.

"I was about ready to give a history lesson on this place. You're just in time," Darci said.

"Or early. Depends on how you look at it," Chloe quipped.

"Here's the short version. In the mid-1900s, Roy Torrens, the man the falls are named after, moved to the area. There was no place for work."

"There's no place for work in this day and age," Chloe said.

Darci sent her a disapproving glare.

"Sorry. Keep going," Chloe said.

"As I was saying, Roy Torrens moved here. Rumor has it he killed one or two people and robbed a bank or two. Then, Roy found a woman who would have him, married her and ended up with a child. He took to fatherhood like a bear to honey. His wife passed, and he became a single parent.

"Somehow, he landed in our fair town. The 1950s was the time to-day's amusement parks started to come into being. Disneyland opened in 1955. So, Roy thought building one here was a good idea."

"Why this place? There's nothing here now. I can't see how there would have been anything decades back," Ken said.

"Decades back, as you say, the land was cheap around here. This land being even less expensive—said to be cursed."

"Okay. Then why build here?" Bart asked.

"Roy seemed to take the cursed land as a challenge. He is famous for saying, 'Let them try to curse me. I'll curse them right back!' And, in the same breath, he said he didn't believe in all this mumbo jumbo.

"Roy thought, like the movie *Field of Dreams*, build it, and they will come. And guess what? They did. People from Louisiana, Texas, and as far east as North Carolina came. When he opened this place in 1960, it was a success."

"So, what happened?" Kat asked. "This place has been abandoned for how long?"

"About twenty years, give or take a few. The place started to fail right after it opened—maybe before. The age-old forewarnings of bad times. The brand-new rides broke. Once, people got stuck in the haunt-ed house," Darci pointed up the hill where a lone spire stuck up through the trees. "They were locked in there for hours. The attraction opera-tor decided to take the afternoon off for no apparent reason, so no one heard the calls for help. By the time someone figured out something was wrong, an old man died of a heart attack from the stress. Later some woman named Martha, I think, fell to her death from the second floor. This Martha was a second fall resulting in death reported at the haunted house. So, this made three."

"The next year, Roy reopened Andalusia Forest. A woman hanged herself in front of the Spider House. Right on the web. Mishaps and deaths continued. And—as an aside—the place continued to succeed. Finally, around 1995, a child went missing and was never found. The po-lice were called in, and they found a jacket, her favorite doll, and her right sneaker. The official report is an abduction."

"And the unofficial report?" Kat asked.

"Well, the land is cursed, is the usual excuse."

"So, why are you here now?" Bart queried.

"A friend—more of an acquaintance—was last reported to be coming up here. He's been gone for four days," Chloe said.

"Did you call the authorities?" Ken asked.

Chloe shook her head.

"Why not?"

"It's complicated. Suffice it to say, the missing guy wasn't here just to take in the sites."

"Explain," Ken said.

"He's not the most law-abiding citizen. He was up here to help himself . . ."

"Why is Jet here?" Darci asked.

"What?" Chloe turned.

A tall, muscular man strode toward the team.

"Great! I'll be right back."

Chloe intercepted Jet. "Thought you weren't coming until AFTER we told you the place isn't haunted."

Jet shrugged. "I changed my mind."

"That's obvious. We don't need the hebe-geebies added to an already creepy location. And you are prone to them. So, why?"

"Because I can't sit around and wait. I'm not good at waiting."

"Work on a car."

"NO."

"You're afraid Shank found something valuable, and you'll be left out, aren't you?"

"I'm not!"

Chloe narrowed her sky-blue eyes and stared into Jet's chocolate-brown eyes. "Look me in the eye and say it."

Jet locked his gaze onto Chloe's, then glanced to the side.

"Ha! I knew it."

"It's only part of the reason," Jet mumbled.

"The other part?"

"He is my friend, and I'm worried."

Chloe took a deep breath. "Fine. The first time you start screaming like a little girl, you are out of here. Understood?"

"Understood," Jet said.

Chloe spun around and marched toward her friends.

A thumb-sized, winged humanoid grinned at the heated exchange. "We've got a keeper," Perse told his companion, Evikal.

"A real keeper," Evikal said. "Cormorant will be pleased."

They flew into the low-lying brush.

"Did you hear that?" Jet said.

"What?" Chloe asked.

"A child laughing. Didn't you hear it?"

"Not a good beginning." Chloe shook her head and jogged to catch up with the others.

CHAPTER 6

"Who do you know to get you in here? And within hours, I might add."

Chloe squinted to read the name tag on the khaki-brown shirt. "Well, Ms. Ortez…"

"Mrs. Ortez."

"Ok, Mrs. Ortez, the current owner…"

"The current owner is my father. I'm Darci." Darci Ludholtz held out her hand to the security guard.

"Oh." Mrs. Ortez took Darci's hand and gave it a tentative shake.

"You understand we can't guarantee your safety? These structures have been vacant for years."

"We understand we are entering at our own risk," Chloe said. "If we didn't already know, those signs dispel any lingering questions." Chloe directed their attention to the padlocked gate at the park's entrance.

Two signs, three feet by three feet each, were staked on either side of the opening. "Private Property. No trespassing. Violators will be prosecuted." And, the worst sign, "If you choose to ignore the first sign, please leave emergency contact information. We will make sure your body gets to the proper relatives."

"Yeah. Roy Torrens' idea. Thought it would keep out the thrill seekers."

"Did it?" Darci asked.

"I'm sure some. Not others, though. This place has seen its share of bloodshed since it closed. Still doesn't stop the curious. You sure you want to do this?" Mrs. Ortez asked.

"Wouldn't be here if we weren't sure," Darci sighed.

"That's true," Chloe chimed in.

"Okay, then." The long-disused padlock creaked in protest against the key, which stopped moving, frozen in the lock. "This is a sticky son of a gator." Mrs. Ortez took hold of the key and twisted it with both hands. The lock popped open, and the rusty chain fell to the ground with a *plop*.

"I'll be back at dusk." Mrs. Ortez looked at her watch. "Which is around 8 o'clock. Be at the gate, or you won't be getting out."

"Man, she's moving like the Grim Reaper is after her," Chloe commented as the stocky woman jogged down the footpath.

"Can't say as I blame her," Darci said. "This place looks like something out of a Stephen King novel."

Chloe took in the neglected gravel footpath. Tendrils of St. Augustine grass crisscrossed the trail like hundreds of small, grass-green snakes. Needle-shaped blades of vegetation jutted skyward like minuscule swords. Gnarled oak trees edged both sides of the pathway.

"Those trees could use some help," Darci said.

"No kidding," Kat interjected. She pointed at a driftwood-grey trunk of one of the trees. "It's been dead for a long time. And everything around it is, too. I'm surprised there hasn't been a wildfire here."

"We have lots of rain," Darci said. "We best keep moving forward. We only have a few hours before we need to be back at the gate."

"Right."

"What is that?" Bart focused on a structure built to look like a tree. Its black trunk, blistered from the heat of many East Texas summers, made it look like it had chicken pox. A face the height of the tree protruded from the trunk. The typical black, angular witch's hat sat over a green, elongated face with a sharp nose and faded blood-red eyes.

"It's even more disturbing up close," Chloe remarked.

"To answer your question, it's one of the first adventures a child would experience in this place," Darci said.

"Explain?" Ken said.

"It's a rendition of Hansel and Gretel. The witch's mouth is the door. See?" Darci walked over and pulled on a thick rope attached to a tooth. A sharp groan, and the mouth opened into a doorway.

"The thing of nightmares. And this place is for kids?" Bart asked.

"The rumor is Roy didn't have a lot of love for kids. Except for his own. And his feelings may have been more obsession than love."

Kat jumped at a sharp *crack,* followed by a muted *thud* to her left. "What was that?"

Darci walked to the edge of the trail. She picked up a dark, round object.

"Let me look at it." Jet snatched the ball from her hand. "This is Shank's! It's a stupid bouncy ball he had as a kid. Called it his good luck charm."

"Shank!" Chloe screamed.

"Shank. We're here for you, man." Jet ran for the deep woods.

"Woah, partner." Ken caught hold of his arm. "You don't know who or what is out there."

Jet yanked his arm free. "Don't touch the goods, man."

Ken reached for Jet again.

Bart stepped forward and put his hand on Ken's forearm. Bart stood, legs apart, thumb on his belt. "You will ALL stay right here, understood? Melbourne and I will take a look."

When they were out of earshot, Ken said, "I don't like this. There is a familiar heaviness."

"Like when Iconoclast was around?"

"Yeah."

"I don't want to jump to conclusions, and maybe it's nerves, but I agree with you. Of course, there isn't much I can think of which trumps the spooky factor of an abandoned, rusting, decaying amusement park," Bart said.

"True. But to be sure," Ken produced a gun from his waistband.

"What are you thinking? We aren't in Alaska. We don't have authority here."

"We have a right to protect ourselves, no matter where we are. There could be wild animals."

"Once an FBI agent, always an FBI agent." Bart bent over and pulled a small .22 caliber revolver from his sock.

Ken smirked. "What's your excuse?"

"Law enforcement never leaves the blood."

Chapter 7

"I hate waiting," Chloe said.

"Who are they to tell us what to do?" Darci asked.

"They are two members from the law enforcement community who first think to protect others. And become almost obsessed when it comes to protecting those they love," Kat said.

"Phhh," Jet said. "That's hogwash. I'm going to look into the stupid witch tree house. Shank probably started there."

"Wait! I'm going with you. We are here to document evidence, after all," Darci said, grabbing a camera and patting her jacket. She smiled and pulled a digital voice recorder from the pocket. "Let's go."

"Don't either of you dare go any farther than the hut!" Chloe demanded. "Shout if you need help."

"Okay. Okay, Mom," Darci said.

"Ken is going to be beyond angry," Kat said.

"We're still here."

"True. And I can't just stand here. How about we scour the ground for something to give us a clue as to your friend Shank's whereabouts?"

Chloe walked fifty feet up the rough lane.

Kat lagged behind, examining each side of the trail.

"Here." Kat snatched a black-handled switchblade out of the tall grass. "Is this Shank's?"

"I'm not sure. It looks like something he'd carry."

"I'll keep it close."

Chloe frowned.

"What's the matter?"

"Knowing Shank, and if the knife is his, he wouldn't have dropped it unless someone made him. He would have used it to defend himself. If something happened, that is."

"Not a good omen," Kat answered.

Kat studied the ground around where she'd found the knife. She picked up a bottle of *Lone Star* beer.

"That's what Shank drinks," Chloe confirmed.

"Alright. Let's go back and wait for Bart and Ken. Then we'll start the search in earnest."

"What about Darci and Jet?"

"I'll go find them," Chloe said.

"I don't want you going anywhere on your own."

"The Old Witch House is right there." Chloe cocked her head to the area behind her. "You can watch me go in."

Kat thought. "Okay. But I'm coming after you if you aren't back with Jet and Darci in ten minutes."

"Deal." Chloe jogged to the structure.

Kat felt a cold breeze whip around her. She shivered. *Just nerves,* she thought.

A low, threatening laugh echoed through the frigid wind. Kat straightened, scanning the landscape for the author of the laughter. *Or not.*

CHAPTER 8

"Jet? Darci?" Chloe called out into the musty-smelling witch's mouth.

A tomb-like silence replied. Chloe stepped into the structure, jammed her boot against the threshold, and fell face down onto the roughhewn floorboards.

"Flashlight, Chloe," she said to herself aloud.

The beam of light illuminated specks of dust and a dark shape in the midst.

"Oh, you've got to go." Chloe dropped her light.

The beam highlighted a tiny, black arachnid—the tale-tell red hourglass on its back announcing a Black Widow.

Chloe jumped up from the floor and backward. Her boot came down with a *Thud* on the spider.

"Jet! Darci! Where in the name of heaven are you?" Chloe shouted.

"Hush."

Chloe directed the beam in the direction of the sound.

A faded mural depicting a small boy and girl walking through candy cane trees and gumdrop flowers met her eyes. In the distance, A gingerbread house, topped with white icing and a gumdrop roof, mimicked the walk. A second mural showed the same children heading onto the gingerbread porch of the cabin.

In a third, the door opened, and a sweet-looking, grandmotherly figure held a plate of fresh baked goods in her hands, inviting the children to eat.

The fourth mural showed the children in a cage. The grandmotherly figure was no more, and a typical evil-looking witch stood hands together, gloating over her 'fresh meat.'

Chloe shivered. "I'll say it again. I never liked the story of Hansel and Gretel. Yuck. Cannibalism. A horror story, maybe. A Fairytale? No."

"Hush!"

Chloe followed the beam of light into the next room.

"I'm getting something here," Darci whispered. "Be quiet!"

Chloe nodded, tiptoed to Darci, and whispered, "Where's Jet?"

Darci pointed toward a third room with her head. She tapped her recorder's *On* button. "Listen to this!"

Chloe leaned toward the recorder. "Listen to what? All I hear are clicks and white noise."

"Just wait!"

Chloe leaned in farther.

A snarl, followed by a rumbling growl, echoed throughout the room. A gravelly voice sent Chloe backward into an upright position. She turned saucer-shaped eyes to Darci. "What can make that noise?"

"Wait."

Chloe leaned in again.

"Welcome." A gravelly voice said. A sinister chuckle followed the greeting.

Goosebumps popped out on Chloe's arms. She backed away from the recorder, shaking her head. "This is not good."

"All the signs of a malevolent haunting, huh?"

"Yep. The growls point toward it, for sure. Anything else?"

"Not yet."

"We need to head back. I'll round up Jet." Chloe walked into the next room.

Jet stared at a black, iron-barred cage. The remnants of two life-size dolls sat inside.

"Now that's plain disturbing," Chloe said.

"I swear they looked at me," Jet said, not turning his eyes from the cage.

"They don't have eyes, Jet."

"They did."

"We need to get you out of here. Your imagination is working over time."

"They had yellow, glowing eyes."

Chloe squeezed his arm. "Look at me."

Jet stared straight ahead.

Chloe shook Jet's arm. "Look at me!"

Jet turned his eyes to Chloe.

"Good. Forget about the dolls. Look at this." Chloe held out the ebony-handled switchblade. "Is this Shank's?"

Jet took the knife from Chloe's hand and turned it over. "Yes!"

"How do you know?"

Jet focused on the initials scratched into the back.

Chloe squinted at the small carving. "SG," she whispered. "Shank Groober."

Jet nodded. "Where did you find this?"

"Kat found it on the trail about fifty feet from here."

A bright look returned to Jet's eyes.

"He'd never let this out of his sight. He has to be in trouble." Jet took off for the entrance to the building.

"Slow down!" Chloe shouted and took off after him. "Come on, Darci," Chloe yelled over her shoulder.

"What's the all-fired hurry?" Darci asked, racing to catch up.

"Found Shank's knife. He never lets it out of his sight. Jet says he's in trouble," Chloe said.

"Wow! Something IS here, and IT got Shank!" Darci said.

Chloe sighed. "And, once again, control of an investigation is lost."

CHAPTER 9

Ken and Bart stood in front of a white nylon spiderweb. Frosted plastic droplets dotted the web like morning dew.

"How many crazy things are there in this place?" Bart asked.

"Worst child's attraction I've ever witnessed," Ken said.

"What kind of parents would bring a kid here?"

"Gothic parents, I guess."

"Ok. So, where's the spider?"

"Good question. Maybe it rotted in the last twenty years."

"I'll go with your thinking. I don't want to see a spider, real or otherwise, who could build this size of a web."

"With you on that, Brother."

Ken stepped to the back of the web. "There's a cave back here."

"Why would someone want access to a cave from this particular building?"

"Good question. Look." Ken said.

Bart stared at the opening. Only black absorbing the light greeted his eyes. "Visions of Ravens Cove, Brother."

Bart thought back to Raven's Ravine and the cavern at the bottom of it. He remembered Iconoclast, the battles fought to save Ravens Cove and all his loved ones, and the lost souls he couldn't save.

Almost reading his thoughts, Ken said, "Iconoclast is gone. This is just a spooky cavern."

Bart nodded. "Right." He stepped forward and peered into the dark. Bart took a flashlight from his belt and shined it around the rocks. "It looks manmade."

"How can you tell?"

"Farther in, I see two-by-fours and chicken coup netting."

Ken walked up beside Bart. "Wow. It looks like a giant Paper Mache rock."

Bart swept the light from side to side. "It's an empty building. With lots of cobwebs."

"There's a bit more than cobwebs here."

"Like what?"

Ken stooped and picked up a large bone. "Like skeletal remains."

"Oh, fudgesicles!" Bart sidled up beside Ken. "Maybe a large animal?"

"Nope."

Bart scanned the cave. His light came to rest on a skull. "Definitely not animal."

"Nope."

"There are more than a few."

"Yep."

"Can you add anything other than a monosyllabic response?"

Ken shrugged. "Looks like we need to call in the authorities. I think this may solve a missing person case or ten."

"Likely." Bart pulled his cell phone from its holster on his belt, dialed 9-1-1, and brought it to his ear. He stared at the phone. "No signal."

"Great. Maybe this rock is shielding the signal. Let's try outside."

They walked to the entrance. A cold wind blasted Ken and Bart from behind, sending chills up their spines.

"Where in the name of heaven did a breeze come from?" Ken asked.

"I have no idea and don't like it," Bart replied. "Let's go back to the trail and make the call from there."

CHAPTER 10

"There you are! I was getting worried," Kat said. She looked at the creases on Ken's face. "What's wrong?"

"We found some bones."

"What kind of bones?" Chloe asked.

"Human ones."

"I knew it! Where?" Jet started into the woods.

Bart jogged past Jet, whirled on his heel, and faced him. "You don't want to go in there alone. And, to answer your question, no, it is not your friend."

"How do you know?"

"Because they are only bones. Shank hasn't been here long enough."

"Yeah, well, he could be in trouble. We need to find him," Chloe responded.

"Not yet," Kat said. "You are foolish to go wandering off."

"They did," Chloe said in a childish whine.

"THEY are experienced police officers. And Bart is an experienced wilderness traveler."

"What's over there?" Darci asked and started up the small gravel trail.

"Hold up." Chloe raced after her.

"And, again, no one listens." Ken said. "What part of stay together don't you understand?" He took off after them.

Darci stopped. "I'm sure I saw something up there."

"Saw what?"

"Look. The place is playing tricks on me. It was nothing."

"Let us decide," Ken said.

"Fine. You'll think I'm nuts. I saw a bush move. No one is there. All I found are some small, cloven hoof prints."

The blood drained from Bart's face. "Cloven hoof prints?"

"Yeah. Like a small goat. But we don't have any wild animals with those prints around here."

"Maybe someone's pet is loose," Chloe commented.

"Maybe," Darci said.

Ken narrowed his eyes. "What else?"

Darci stared at her hands. She reached into his pocket and pulled out some silver fur. "I found this. I thought I saw bright gold eyes in the woods—staring at me. I'm telling you, I'm being hyper-imaginative right now. There is nothing around here with silver fur and gold eyes."

"There are coyotes," Chloe said.

"I guess," Darci said.

"The Kumrande," Bart and Ken said at the same time.

Kat's eyes grew wide. "It can't be them. They were destroyed by Pet himself."

"Who are the Kumrande? Who is Pet?" Chloe asked.

"They are two of several reasons I don't let these two"—Bart pointed to Kat and Ken— "go anywhere without me."

"Buddy, you need to understand. My friend is here, and I need to know what we are up against." Jet folded his arms across his chest and glared at Bart.

"Buddy, you better rethink your alpha male stance," Bart growled. He stood, legs planted slightly apart and his hand on his belt.

Kat saw the signs of a war about to erupt. She stepped between Bart and Jet. "That's enough. Stand down, you two."

Chloe placed her hand on Jet's arm. "Stop it. If you want our help, you'd better behave. Even if you don't know how to."

Jet inhaled, then mumbled, "For now."

"Right," Bart relaxed.

"The Kumrande are, well, for lack of a better term, mythical creatures. But, as we discovered, they are not mythical at all. They are maneaters and serve demons."

"And I thought Chloe could imagine some crazy stuff," Darci said.

"Young lady, we have been where you are. We have denied anything supernatural existed. I almost died because of it." Bart's mind raced back to the night he sat in a puddle at his front door, studying his .357-gun barrel, deciding when to pull the trigger. He remembered hearing people in the distance—Ken, Kat, and Pastor Paul Lucas, to be exact. They laid hands on him and prayed in Jesus' name. A black mist came out of him—a possession Paul Lucas said.

"We all almost died because of it," Kat said.

"Ok. So who is Pet?"

"One of the most innocent-looking and deadly demons from hell," Kat said. She shivered, remembering almost being taken to the cave in Ravens Ravine as Iconoclast's latest sacrifice.

"Good to know. We'll keep an eye out," Darci said.

"This is not funny, Darci. This is life and death. It is spiritual life and death. If the Kumrande are here, they have been called out by a demon. No one else can bring them. If you have a demon in this place, it is just waiting to consume as many souls as possible. It will use any means to do it," Ken said.

"Right. Well, I don't believe in such things," Darci said.

"I can't say as I do either, Ken," Chloe said.

"You don't have to understand. But, Pip Squeak, you better believe me."

"It doesn't matter who or what is here. We just need to find Shank and vacate this place before sundown," Jet said.

"We have plenty of time," Darci responded.

"Take us to where you saw the hoof prints," Ken said.

The small crew made their way up the overgrown pathway.

Chloe took in the macabre decorations. Four-foot-tall statues of fairies stood on her left, dancing around a faded red and white specked mushroom. On her left stood a tall statue of a grey wolf, standing on two feet with eyeglasses and a shawl as decoration.

"Man, this place even gives the little people a bad name," she said. "And, if that's not enough, the typical Big Bad Wolf looks ready to pounce."

"Well, in some stories, pixies aren't good. They are mean creatures bent on man's destruction," Darci said.

"Ever the historian."

"That's my job. "You know what's weird?" Darci asked.

"No."

"This place has been closed for twenty years. These buildings and statues shouldn't be standing. The humidity and heat turn metal to rust and wood to splinters in a few years," Darci said.

Chloe scrutinized a dark grey Victorian-style house on a hill. "The mansion looks like it was built yesterday."

Kat took her hand. "Maybe it will look more dated when we get closer."

"Maybe," Chloe said.

"This place is getting to all of us. Stupid urban legends. The power of suggestion is alive and well," Jet said.

Darci stopped. "Here."

Bart sat on his heels. "Oh, man."

Ken looked down and shook his head. "Sure looks like the Kumrande."

"If so, we need to be out of here before nightfall," Kat said.

"Why?" Darci asked. "Those prints are pint-sized. I could take this animal and not break a sweat."

"Those feet, together with flesh-tearing teeth and claws and their favorite poison in a blow gun, will take you down in a few seconds," Bart replied.

"Oh."

Kat looked up to the sky. "The sun is low. What time is it?"

"My watch says six o'clock," Darci said.

"The sky says much later," Bart replied.

"You're right. We better go back to the entrance."

"We are not leaving Shank," Jet said.

"We will come back tomorrow for him," Chloe said.

"Tomorrow may be too late."

"We can't stay into the night."

"Doesn't look like we have a choice," Kat said.

"Why?"

"I have no cell phone signal, but I do have the time." She held it up for Chloe. "It says it's eight-thirty. We've missed our chance to leave tonight."

"What the—? How?" Darci looked at her watch again. "It says six-ten."

"It's wrong."

"Let's hope Mrs. Ortez waited a few minutes. Let's go—NOW.

———————

Perse grinned. "How did you do it, Evikal?"

"Road kill has its advantages," Evikal retorted.

"How so?"

"Take some gray moss and mix it with coyote fur, and it appears to be silver—especially to a terrified human. Then, add a hoof print from a young, dead deer, and you have their worst fear—a Kumrande."

"How did you discover their meeting with the Kumrande?"

"Lucius's knowledge is vast. He instructed me on them. I did the rest." Evikal's chest puffed out in pride.

"And the eyes?"

"Ahh. A bit harder to recreate. But broken bottles litter the surrounding areas. It was easy to find the gold color. I propped them up in the sunlight. I didn't know if it would work. But, it did."

"Their imaginations filled in the gaps," Perse said.

"Oh, what fun. Humans filled with terror are so easy to take down."

"Indeed."

CHAPTER 11

Chloe reached Andalusia Forest's entrance as the sun melted below the skyline, dusk settling like an indigo blanket over the landscape.

A fragment of paper fluttered in the night breeze. She ripped the note from the blue gate.

She read aloud, "*Can't wait any longer. Back at sunrise. Mrs. O.*"

"Now what?" Kat asked.

"Did anyone bring food?" Jet said.

"Seriously, Jet? We're stuck in this place, and you are worried about your stomach?" Chloe said.

Jet shrugged.

"I always have snacks." Darci reached into her backpack and produced several energy bars.

"Well, those will do for tonight," Kat said.

"Where are we going to sleep?" Chloe asked

"I, for one, won't be sleeping," Ken said.

"Sleep or not, we need a place to hunker down and one where we will see what's coming in the night," Kat said.

"Point taken," Bart said.

"There's some kind of office building off the right of the path, up there," Darci said.

"How do you discover it?"

"Researched the place, remember?"

"Ok. We need to get there before complete nightfall."

Chloe, Kat, Ken, Bart, Jet, and Darci retraced their steps on the overgrown trail.

"This place is taking on a major creep factor now," Darci said.

Chloe focused on the trees lining the pathway. It was a moonless night, but she could make out the branches dotted with clumps of leaves. They looked like tangled webs of fur. When they shook in the evening breeze, they almost moaned.

Up the trail, by the fairy statues, the mushroom seemed to emit its own light. The sprites' faces glowed. Their lips curled up in a menacing smile. Their eyes were small slits, black, vacant irises focused on the trail.

The wolf, directly across from the dancing nymphs, sneered, baring fanged teeth. His glasses reflected the ethereal light from the mushroom. The large, amber-colored eyes danced with life in the beam.

"Creepier than I thought it could be," Chloe said.

"I'm going after Shank!" Jet said. "Dark or not."

"Your precious treasure, if he found anything, will be with him tomorrow morning."

"I'm not worried about what he found. I'm worried about him."

"You're scared of Shank and what he'll do to you if he finds out you left him here."

"I am not!"

"Yes, you are."

A loud *crack* from behind a dead oak emphasized the menacing atmosphere of Andalusia Forest.

Jet jumped. "Shank?"

"Told you."

"Stop acting like children, both of you," Ken said. "We need to find shelter.

"Here's where we turn off," Darci said.

"That's pretty dense."

"It's either go for the office or go up the hill to the house." Darci pointed at the Victorian looming above them.

Ken scanned the malevolent outline of the structure. "Alright. The office it is. Lead on."

Darci took a step onto the dirt. A hiss greeted her. She jumped backward. "There's something in the underbrush."

Ken flicked on the LED light and scanned the shrubbery. A red, yellow, and black striped snake lay to the right of the trail.

"That's not good. It's a coral. They are poisonous," Darci said.

Chloe grabbed a long stick from the pathway. She thrust it at the snake. It slithered away into the brush. "They are more afraid of us than we are of them. Come on."

"I'm not sure that's true." Ken crept ahead, scanning the trail carefully.

"I'll feel better when we find the office. Being out in the dark in this place is not my idea of a good time," Kat said.

"I hear you," Darci said.

The troupe navigated the narrow space in silence. Farther in, the tall trees and underbrush choked the pathway into a dusty line.

"I thought we were giving this spooky stuff a break," Bart said.

"Right now, it's just a dark, creepy forest. Nothing too spooky," Kat said.

A pair of golden eyes glittered to Ken's left. He swung his flashlight in their direction. "What in the name of all that's Holy is that?"

Bart focused his beam in Ken's direction.

Ken covered his eyes. "Blinding me here."

"Sorry." Bart directed the light toward the underbrush. A light piece of fur fluttered in the breeze.

"Looks like some type of animal hair," Chloe commented.

"Yeah. It does." Bart held the fur up to Ken.

"We had better find shelter and find it now!"

"Why?"

"That's Kumrande fur."

"Don't be silly. The Kumrande were in Alaska. Not here," Kat reminded Ken.

"Maybe Alaska doesn't have complete ownership rights on them."

"They serve demons. Demons are all over the world, right?"

"Right," Kat said. "Let's move."

"Here we are," Darci said.

A small brown-board building greeted them. Sage-green moss and dark leaves clung to the hut's green asphalt shingles.

Chloe walked to a six-panel window and peeked inside. "Not much in there. Lots of cobwebs. And ancient-looking equipment of some kind."

"Let's go inside."

The door opened with a gentle tug.

"Guess no one is afraid of being vandalized here," Darci commented.

"Anything of value is long gone by now," Chloe said.

They meandered into the shack. Dust billowed up with each footstep, filling the light beams like a glittering fog.

A rough-hewn bench sat across from the small window, and an L-shaped table was positioned beneath the window and to the left side of the cabin.

Kat perused the old magazines and papers littering the makeshift desk. "Nothing here of interest."

"At least it's shelter," Darci said.

"Now, if we can make it until morning in one piece," Ken said.

"Amen," Bart answered. "And, again, I say Amen."

CHAPTER 12

Kat drifted into a fitful sleep, dreaming of crimson eyes and clawed, leathery fingers.

A loud *thwack* reverberated throughout the building, shaking the window.

Kat jumped up from the old wood bench. "Now what?"

"Good question," Bart said, swinging the beam toward the window.

Ken strode to the door, "One way to find out."

"No!" Chloe, Darci, and Jet said in unison.

"It could have been your friend," Ken said.

"I vote we all go," Kat said.

"No."

"Well, you aren't going by yourself."

"Fair enough. Coming Bart?"

"Thought you'd never ask."

Bart and Ken picked up the LED flashlights and stepped into the late-night darkness.

Bart swung his light from right to left and back again. "Where did this fog come from?"

"Another good question," Ken said.

The beam bounced off the smokey mist, making it impossible to discern what lay a few feet ahead.

"Gonna be hard to make our way anywhere at this rate," Ken said.

Bart scanned the dirt outside the office wall with the light. He crouched. "Look at this."

Ken studied the markings. "Huh."

"Those are the weirdest tracks I've ever seen," Bart said.

"I'm hoping this is someone's idea of a practical joke. Maybe Mrs. Ortiz has a strange sense of humor? Or someone else who wants us to think this place is haunted?" Ken asked.

"Maybe. The tracks almost look like someone dug a rounded dowel into the earth."

"This lady will have something to answer for if it is her." Ken turned and started up the trail, following the deep, rounded indentations.

The holes crossed the dirt trail and continued into the brush and shrubs.

"Would you look at the bushes?" Bart directed Ken's attention to broken branches and flattened grass.

"Yeah. Something big made its way through there." Ken strode onto the packed vegetation.

Bart gripped his arm. "Woah. What do you think you're doing? Whatever made those tracks is huge. Are you gonna fight it with your bare hands? Maybe throw one of your boots at it? We need to regroup."

"Flashlights worked on the Kumrande," Ken said.

Bart shivered at remembering the grey, fur-covered creatures with yellow, intelligent eyes circling him and Ken. They emptied their guns, and it didn't affect the nasty critters. When Ken went to use his flashlight as a club, he flipped it on, too. The LED lights blinded the Kumrande, and they took off.

"I don't think I've ever heard a more satisfying screech than when those nasty creatures were blinded by the beam of light," Bart said.

"Not to mention the relief. I thought we were goners for sure."

"I don't think we'd be so lucky twice, Brother."

"What do you suggest?"

"We tiptoe so as not to alert whatever this is."

"Might lead us to Shank."

"I hope not; that would tell me Shank is quite possibly no longer among the living."

Ken started forward, following the broken branches on low-lying trees and flattened shrubs.

Bart followed.

Ken stepped out onto an overgrown lawn. "Great. This makes the night better."

Bart looked up at an old Victorian House. "Looks like the Bates Motel out of *Psycho*."

"Worse, I think. I'm guessing this was the haunted house attraction?"

"Guessing."

"The tracks stop here. Where could the thing have gone?"

"Don't know. My question is, what kind of thing are we dealing with?"

"I didn't realize this was so close to the office. I wonder if a vagrant or someone is living here."

"No human made those tracks."

"Should we take a look?"

"Maybe . . . "

"You're going to take a look without us?" Kat shouted from behind them.

Bart wheeled 180 degrees in one movement. "We told you guys to stay put."

One by one, Chloe, Jet, and Darci stepped up beside Kat.

"This is my investigation, Ken!" Chloe said.

"You are my blood, and I'm responsible for you. Back to the office. All of you," Ken commanded.

"Not happening," Kat responded. "Besides, you might need this." Kat pulled a gun out of her pocket.

"How did you get a firearm in here?"

"I have my ways," Kat said.

"You are so on my bad list, Kat. It's against the law to carry a gun and not have a permit!" Ken reminded her.

"I don't need a permit. I'm from Alaska."

"Not the same!"

Kat shrugged. "Tomato, Tamato."

Ire worked its way up from Ken's stomach to his heart and brain. "You are impossible and reckless!"

"And you're a fool if you think I'm going into these woods without protection," Kat said.

"Stop. You will bring that creature down on us," Bart said.

Kat relaxed. "Fine. This isn't over, FBI." Kat used the term she always used with Ken when angry at him.

"Fine. Ice Queen," Ken retorted.

"What is wrong with you two?" Chloe asked. "I'm never getting married."

"They love each other and are devoted to each other. They just don't understand how to be cordial all the time," Bart said. "That's why I'm along — to keep them civil and out of paranormal trouble."

"Hey guys," Jet said.

"What?" Chloe snarled.

"What is the orange glow in the second floor's front window?" Jet asked. "Isn't this place abandoned?"

"It looks like someone left a light on for us."

"You're such a comedian, Darci," Chloe said.

"You all stay here; Bart and I will go take a look," Ken said.

"Thanks for volunteering me again, Brother."

"You're more than welcome."

"What are we supposed to do?" Kat asked.

"Go back to the office. We will come to get you when we are done."

"That's not happening," Kat said.

"Fine. I don't care what you do. Just stay out of trouble and don't follow us in."

––––––––

Small, purple-flecked eyes tracked Bart and Ken as they made their way up the steps of the haunted house.

The fairy, named Perse, grinned. "Oh, this will be fun. Wait until they are inside. They will wish they never came to Andalusia Forest."

Miniature moth-like wings unfolded on the elfin-like back. A slight buzz, which sounded like a small jet revving its engine, preceded Perse's departure.

CHAPTER 13

Bart and Ken strode up the disfigured steps of the porch. One plank groaned under Ken's weight.

"Might want to consider a diet, married man."

"Ha! I don't weigh any more than when you first met me."

Bart looked at the slight belly protruding over Ken's belt. "If you say so."

A faded, blistered, red-painted door greeted them. A musty odor, like long-decaying leaves, assaulted Ken's senses.

"You smell that?"

"Yeah. Where is it coming from?"

Ken swung the light around and swept left and right on the porch. "There."

His light stopped atop a large mound of dirt, squirming with life.

Bart turned his attention to the mound. "Oh, tell me this is a nightmare."

"Snakes. Lots of snakes."

"Oh, for the love of Pete, those are garden snakes," Chloe said from behind Ken.

"What are you doing up here?"

"Educating my big, scaredy cat relative and his Alaska friend on the local reptiles," Chloe quipped.

Ken turned and pointed to the pathway. "Go!"

"Kat thought you might like this," Chloe held out her hand. Another gun sat in it.

Ken closed his eyes and took a breath. "How?"

"She said it's as easy to smuggle two as one." Chloe turned and walked down the porch steps.

"Always the ingenious one, our Kat." Bart took the gun from Ken.

"Don't suppose you're going to tell her we already have our fire-arms, huh?"

"Definitely not. But I'm going to have a long talk with her—and, then . . ."

"Right, Brother, then you're going to sleep on a couch for a month." Bart chuckled. "Let's go in."

The red door squealed.

"I'd say this hasn't been opened in decades."

"I'd say you are right, but the light?"

"True."

Ken stepped over to the once ornate staircase. "This is going to be tricky." He pointed mid-way up. Two stair treads hung in the air, swinging in a non-existent breeze.

"Never easy," Bart said.

Ken scanned the room. "This'll work." He snagged an old dust cover from a couch.

"How convenient. I guess someone thought they were coming back—decades ago."

Bart took the dust cover and yanked hard with both hands. "It's sturdy. If we can make it up, we can use this to come back down."

Ken scrutinized the small chasm. He leaped to the step above. It creaked and groaned under his weight. He jogged up the remaining stairs to the landing.

Bart followed. He turned when the last stair split with a sharp *crack* and dropped from the riser to the foyer. "Don't know if the dust cover will work to get us down."

"We'll worry about it later. Let's keep moving."

Bart and Ken picked their way from the open loft area to a darkened hallway. Orange light glowed through the last door on the left.

Ken stopped in front of one of the numerous old paintings and tap-estries lining the hallway.

It depicted a grassy meadow surrounded by tall, thin evergreens. Shrubs dotted the area between the statuesque trees. A tripod with an aqua-blue pendant dangling over a pond sat in the middle of the grassland.

"Where and what does this represent?" Ken asked.

Bart studied the painting. The chain swayed right and left, as in a strong wind. He closed his eyes and opened them again. The necklace stayed still. *My imagination is working overtime.* He thought.

"Maybe it's someone's idea of art." Bart moved toward the light.

Ken swatted at his face. "Dang bugs!"

"Ouch!" Bart slapped his arm. He looked down at his right hand. Blood oozed from a narrow puncture wound. "What insect draws this much blood?"

Ken whacked his legs, then arms. "What kind of nasty insects are in this place?"

Bart snatched up one of the bugs attacking him. He opened his hand and caught sight of a small, human-type head and wispy wings fluttering at the speed of a hummingbird's. "You aren't going to believe this."

Ken stared at Bart's hand and shook his head. "Once again, I am tired of seeing things which aren't supposed to exist. It looks like a fairy."

"Right, why not? Ouch." Bart batted at his left arm. "Whatever you are, stop it!"

A slight wind, filled with laughter, rushed by Bart's ear.

"Noooo." A little voice said out of the wind.

An army of winged creatures hovered in front of the lighted doorway.

"I guess they don't want us to go in."

"Doesn't seem so," Bart said.

"I don't like being told by a bunch of tiny aliens I can't go somewhere, do you?"

"Nope."

Ken looked around. A dusty iron sat atop a dirty, dark cherry buffet. Next to it a bell in the same metal. "Huh. Wonder why these are here?"

Ken picked up the bell. A clear chime echoed through the still-as-death house.

High-pitched screeches preceded the dispersion of the pygmy-sized battalion. The sound of crickets wafted up the stairs of the previous silent house.

"Who knew? A bell scares off weird little humans with wings," Bart said.

"Well, I did read somewhere fairies don't like iron, and they detest chimes."

"Light reading?"

"You never know what you are going to come up against, right?"

"Right. Moving on."

Bart and Ken made their way to the glowing room. The light dimmed. Complete darkness cloaked the chamber.

Ken released his gun and held it waist-high.

Bart scanned the room with his flashlight.

The light beam danced from one side of the room to another. Nothing seemed unusual except the space itself—spotless and in perfect condition, unlike the staircase and foyer.

Ken strolled into the room, holstering his gun and releasing the spot-light from his belt.

A miniature version of the painting in the hallway sat on the bedside table. This one, however, showed a tall man, rather unearthly looking, grimacing at the pendant, studying it but not trying to retrieve it.

"You don't belong here."

Ken jumped and whirled around to face the voice.

Bart came up beside him.

A misty figure rose from the floorboards until it touched the ceiling.

"You're seeing this, right?" Bart said to Ken out of the corner of his mouth.

Ken nodded, not taking his eyes off the apparition.

The misty figure became solid. It glared at Ken and Bart. "I said you don't belong here. Go!"

Ken and Bart stood their ground. Having recovered their senses, they both turned resolute eyes to the apparition.

"I'm not going anywhere right now. How about you, Bart?"

"Nope. Not feeling it."

The figure, now an older woman with long, grey hair, pointed at them both. An electric-blue spark jumped from her index finger.

Ken and Bart dove in separate directions.

The figure focused on Bart. Light sparked and sizzled on its forefinger.

Bart glanced right, then left for an exit. He scrambled backward and stopped short when he bumped into the corner wall. He tensed in antici-pation of the jolt to come.

A voice, ever so small and yet as loud as thunder, whispered to Ken, "Call on Jesus. Now!"

Ken looked around for the source. No one was there. It sounded familiar, yet he couldn't pinpoint who whispered in his mind.

Ken shrugged, "In the name of Jesus, STOP."

The light from the old woman's figure sputtered, then dissipated.

She turned rageful eyes, flashing with the same electric-blue light on Ken. "What did you say?" She hissed.

Ken's voice, shaking a moment before, came out strong. "I said, stop in the name of Jesus." Ken stood up. "Now."

The being started to twist and twirl. The woman transformed into a black wolf with glittering orange eyes. It bared its teeth and snarled.

Ken released the gun from his belt. He aimed at the wolf.

The wolf threw its head back and howled.

The hair stood at attention on Bart's neck.

The howl ended in a guttural laugh. "Your guns will do nothing to me!"

"That may be true, but the name of Jesus does! In agreement with my Brother, Ken, be gone in the mighty name of JESUS," Bart shouted.

The apparition vibrated, splintering into several white orbs. "We will meet again. This is not over." The spheres dissolved into the floorboards.

Kat's scream reached Ken and Bart.

"Now what?"

Bart ran to the window. He yanked. It didn't open.

Ken took hold of the windowsill. "On three. One, two, three."

Bart and Ken hoisted the sash.

The team below slapped at iridescent flying creatures.

Bart's eyes widened as he witnessed Darci lift off the ground, then drop with a loud *thud.*

The tiny beings grouped together and dove in unison like miniature F-16s.

Darci shrieked and held up her arms to protect her face. As the fairies landed, her shrieks became loud screams.

Ken looked at the bell in his hand. "Kat. Catch!"

Kat caught it in midair. "What am I supposed to do with this? Play a tune?"

"Ring it. Ring it hard and ring it now."

"Okay." Kat moved her hand up and down. The melodic tones filled the night air.

The creatures screeched and retreated to the woodland edge.

Kat smiled. She held her arm high overhead and brought the bell down.

Sharp squeaks rose to Ken and Bart like a branch on a window in a strong wind. The winged humans scattered in all directions.

Ken and Bart made their way back down the broken staircase and out to the lawn of the haunted house.

Darci lay on the ground, moaning.

"All those pinpricks remind me of a voodoo doll," Bart said.

Tiny rivulets of blood covered most of Darci's body.

"She's losing a lot of blood," Ken said.

"Yes. We need to move her inside and stop the bleeding," Kat said.

Chloe stood paralyzed, staring at Darci.

"What are you looking at?" Jet asked Chloe. "You heard the man." Jet gripped Darci under her arms. Droplets of blood ran onto Jet's hands. "I could use some help—now!"

Chloe shook herself and took hold of Darci's feet.

Ken supported her lower back. "Let's get in the house before those blue terrors return."

———————

Purple eyes followed the troupe into the house. Perse grimaced. "I hate humans."

"This is a small setback," Evikal said. It makes our coming victory more glorious."

Perse stared at Evikal. "You make no sense."

"We have lost a battle, not the war," Evikal said.

Perse smiled. "True."

Evikal and Perse flew into the safety of the dark woodland.

CHAPTER 14

Cormorant soared into the grassy land, which surrounded a tripod supporting a necklace over the dark water of a small pond.

"What news do you bring?" A tall, bronze-skinned man asked.

"We have wounded one of the intruders, Lucius."

"Only ONE?" Lucius bellowed. He raised a gnarled hand and swatted. The fairy darted backward, the bronze fingertip grazing his body.

He hovered several yards away from Lucius.

"Yes, we had them all until they rang the Iron Bell!"

Lucius growled. "How did the humans find it?"

"It is a mystery. The bell seemed to appear on a table in the House. It was not there before."

"Who is helping these horrible people? Why didn't Savaniah take care of them?" Lucius spoke of the apparition who appeared to Ken and Bart.

"They called on the Name of the Holy One!"

Lucius roared. The crickets and tree frogs stopped singing. The forest fell dead silent.

A battalion of sprites joined Cormorant. They floated in a ring around Lucius, all a few feet away from the copper-skinned man.

Lucius paced the meadow, then stopped. "Perse, go to the house. Do not be detected. Tell me how the creature you wounded is. If she dies, they will leave, and we can continue. If she lives, we will bring in an army to destroy them. Mildred must not be found out."

"Why? Mildred could destroy them."

"Not if they are strong in The One. Mildred is for another purpose. The world is starting toward a time when she will be useful. Until then, we hide her."

71

"As you say," Perse gave an in-air bow and glided to the mansion.

Lucius looked at the other nymphs. "Call in the Red Caps! And do it NOW."

CHAPTER 15

Kat spotted the old dust cover hanging from the second floor to the staircase. She yanked it to the ground, took an end of the fabric in each hand, and tugged.

"You may be strong, but you aren't going to tear the cloth without help." Jet pulled a switchblade from his pocket.

Kat jumped back as Jet drove the blade into the material, ripping some of the fabric into strips.

"Not the most sanitary, but it's going to have to do for now." Ken wrapped Darci's left arm.

Kat and Bart covered her other arm and legs.

"Do we have any water?" Kat asked.

Ken snagged the water bottle from his backpack and threw it to Kat.

Kat poured the clear liquid on a washcloth-size piece of material and dabbed Darci's face.

"The bleeding is stopping. Darci, how are you?"

Darci moaned. "I feel like I've been stung by a thousand bees. And I can't stop shaking."

"You're in shock." Kat looked around the room. A tapestry lay on the floor, severed years before from its place on the wall. "I'll be right back." Kat dashed out the front door and started shaking the tapestry with all her might.

"Here. Let me help." Ken clutched the opposite end. They shook the wallcovering in unison.

Kat gave Ken a peck on the cheek. "Still my hero, at times, FBI." She smiled at him.

Ken grabbed her and held on tight. "And you are to me, KittyKat," he whispered.

Even in the heat of East Texas, Darci was cold to the touch. They cocooned her in the jacquard material.

Darci stopped shaking. She gave Kat a wan smile.

"Wish I had something strong for you, but all I have is water." Kat held out the bottle.

Jet waved it away. "I've got this." He pulled a silver flask from his left front pocket. "Take a swig. Just one!"

Darci took a big drink. She gasped. Tears cascaded down her cheeks. "Wow. Dare I ask what you just gave me?" Darci said.

"My uncle's moonshine. Best alcohol in the county."

"Best *poison* in the county, you mean." Darci pushed the makeshift blanket below her arms and turned to Chloe.

"Those *things* who attacked me? I'd say they were fairies if I believed in them."

Chloe gave her a questioning look.

Darci held up a hand. "I understand. It's crazy, but they match the description to a T of the ones I researched. And, the bell driving them off also matches what I've read about protection against them."

"I thought fairies were nice, you know, like Tinkerbell in *Peter Pan*," Kat said.

"Their disposition is up for debate," Darci replied.

"I'd say," Bart chimed in. "Why don't we ever run into the nice mythological creatures?"

"Is there such a thing?" Kat asked. "If so, I've never met one." Kat thought back on all the battles with Iconoclast and his demons.

"True. Iconoclast was a legend, too," Ken echoed her thoughts. "He was one nasty piece of work."

"Understatement," Bart said under his breath.

Ken looked out the dirt-covered window. Light rimmed the dark sky. "Looks like the sun's about to come up. Let's find a way to get Darci to the front gate and out of here."

"We haven't found Shank! I'm not leaving him," Jet said.

"We all need to leave! This place is dangerous if you haven't noticed," Chloe said.

"Maybe. But I'm not leaving my friend."

"Darci needs medical help. Afterward, we can regroup and decide what we are doing about Shank," Ken replied.

"Agreed," Kat said.

Chloe locked her eyes on Jet's. "Look, Jet, we can come back tomorrow. We need to be more prepared than we are right now. We are lucky to all still have our lives."

Jet narrowed his eyes. "You promise?"

"Yes," Chloe said.

Bart ripped the dust cover off a nearby chair. He strode to the staircase and yanked two of the loose boards free. "If we put these together, we can carry Darci out."

Bart and Ken set about tying the boards to the dust cover with the remaining pieces of cloth bandages. Jet, Kat, and Chloe placed Darci on the makeshift stretcher.

"Let's head out," Ken said.

They doubled back down the yard and small trail to the office cabin. From there, it was a familiar walk to the front gate.

Mrs. Ortez paced the gate. She zeroed in on Kat. "What happened?"

"It was a bad night. Darci got stung by fairi…something all over. She had a nasty reaction. We need to get her to the hospital."

Mrs. Ortez opened the gate. "Put her in the back of my Jeep. The rest of you follow me."

Mrs. Ortez didn't wait for an answer. She climbed in the Jeep, motioned the guys to hurry, and took off as soon as Darci was settled.

"Man, that woman can move."

"Come on!" Jet shouted. "We've got to come back here as soon as possible. Shank is in trouble. I can feel it in my bones!"

CHAPTER 16

Perse and Evikal scrutinized the cars disappearing in clouds on the dry dirt road.

"This does not bode well," Perse said.

"They are gone. I think it bodes very well," Evikal answered.

Perse landed on the gate and stared into Evikal's eyes. "Did you not hear they are returning?"

Evikal's lavender eyes met Perse's. "Of course I did! But we can be ready for them now, can't we? We can finish all of them before they find out about Lucius—and his secret."

Perse hovered in midair. "True. Their return will be their doom and our victory!"

CHAPTER 17

Chloe dropped her gray and blue backpack. "Welcome to my humble home."

Kat purveyed the living room, only large enough to accommodate a loveseat and matching wing-back chair. Although small, the room was tidy. Instead of feeling closed in, Kat felt blanketed in a cozy atmosphere. She took in a teal blue rug, Tiffany lamps on diminutive end tables, and the print of a blue waterfall cascading into a small pond below. Birds perched on branches of trees beside the pond. The sky was dotted with white clouds. She could almost feel the warmth and hear water splashing as the falls cascaded into the pool.

"It's a lovely home," Kat said.

Chloe beamed. "Thanks. You can stay here if you want. There is a guest bedroom—the size of a closet." She laughed.

"Let's come up with a strategy first. After we have a plan, we'll decide about accommodations," Ken said.

"I'll make some coffee." Chloe disappeared into a doorway to the left of the waterfall print.

Ken turned to Kat. "I'm so sorry about this, Kat. I know you want to go home."

Kat's emerald green eyes locked onto Ken's blue ones. "I do. Yet, I believe we need to be here. You were right to stay."

Ken pulled Kat into his arms. "Do you even comprehend how much I love you?"

Kat grinned. "A little. But you can keep reminding me as much as you want."

Ken kissed Kat long and hard.

Bart dropped a suitcase.

Kat jumped, turned, and glared at Bart.

"Don't give me *the* look! You can play hanky-panky all you want AFTER we are through this current supernatural crisis. Please help me unload the car if you'd be so kind."

"On it!" Ken disappeared outside and returned carrying a large dish and a black laptop bag.

"What 's the plastic dish for?" Kat asked.

Chloe set a silver tray with gold-rimmed cups and a matching pot on the coffee table. "Oh, that's a parabolic listening device. It picks up sounds far away and is helpful in investigations."

"Has anyone updated you on Darci's condition?" Bart asked.

"Not really. She is resting. She lost some blood, not life-threatening, and was dehydrated. They think she can be released tomorrow. But Darci can't go on a hike or do strenuous exercise for at least a week."

"I'm glad she's at the hospital."

"Me, too," Chloe answered. "I don't know what I'd do without her. She is a great friend."

"Now, about tomorrow," Kat said.

"I need to talk to some people. I'm not sure this is such a good idea. Whatever we are dealing with is, well, dangerous. And I'm making an understatement," Chloe said.

"I'm going. Told you I'd be back up there when we left. With or without any of you," Jet said.

"Are you sure Shank stayed in Andalusia Forest?"

"Yeah. He was hot to trot. He said something there would make him rich. He would have come home asap after he got it. His mom needs him."

Ken raised an eyebrow. "Ok. Why aren't we sending in the police?"

Jet stood straight. "Because they will say he is a big boy and may have just taken off. And also, Shank or I, for that matter, don't need the cops poking around."

"I'm a cop, you know."

"True. Maybe you should stay here. We don't need your help."

"Oh, yes, you do," Kat said. "Unless you've dealt with ghosts, demons, and other legendary creatures. Have you?"

"No."

"So, when a ghost decides to make you its permanent home because it's really a demon, how are you going to stop it?"

"It won't. I'm too tough. I'll fight it off."

"Well, if you say so. But I can tell you firsthand those entities are shrewd. I almost ended up dead because they tricked us so easily. Do you want to take a chance? Do you want to risk Chloe's life on your physical power alone?"

"No."

"Ok. We all go." Kat plopped onto the couch and sipped coffee. "First, we need to understand what we're up against."

Chloe snatched a notebook from her backpack. "Darci's fairy research should be in here." Chloe started flipping through the pages.

Chloe dropped the book onto the floor, shaking her head. Her eyes took on a faraway look.

"Chloe?" Ken shook her shoulder. "Chloe!" He said louder.

Chloe turned frightened, glazed eyes to Ken. She picked up and handed him the notebook.

Ken read, "In Scottish stories, the Sluagh, a mythical being in Scottish folklore, is composed of fairies who were thought to be the souls of evil people and those who died without baptism. This malevolent swarm is known to fly at night, fighting amongst themselves and hunting for victims. Any unfortunate target would be attacked by the mob and carried away until the poor soul got dropped from a great height." He stopped. "Was Darci dropped from a great height?"

"No. But those things lifted Darci and dropped her from a small height before we got to her."

"Okay. We may have an idea of what we're dealing with," Bart said. "Is there any way to stop these miniature murderers?"

Ken continued, "The Sluagh also have a penchant for sadism, as they sometimes force the victims to shoot at other people and animals with poisoned arrows. People closed their west-facing windows to fend off the Sluagh since the swarm tended to arrive from that direction.

Their malodorous corpse-like stench also warned the people of their impending arrival."

"You guys are nuts. Darci was attacked by a swarm of nasty insects." Jet crossed his arms and stared at the landscape on Chloe's wall.

"Believe what's easiest for you, Jet. For me, I'm going with the thought they could be fairies. They didn't make her shoot anyone with poison arrows, though," Kat said.

"And I didn't detect a particular stench," Bart said.

"Well, they skedaddled pretty quick when you rang the bell," Chloe remarked. "Who says what would have happened if we hadn't intervened? They were just getting started."

"True," Kat said.

"Good grief, how many legends need to come to life in one man's lifetime?" Ken lamented.

Kat let out a small giggle. "As many as needed, I guess, FBI."

Ken scowled at Kat. "You are so reassuring."

"So, how do we irradicate them?" Bart asked.

"Well, if these are anything like what we've dealt with before, they won't die. Our best hope is to incapacitate them," Bart said.

"The notebook says, 'Although considered somewhat immortal, fairies can die.' They do not die of natural causes, though," Ken said.

"What does that mean?" Chloe asked.

"Well, maybe we can squash them—like the nasty bugs they are," Bart said. "In fact, I like this idea."

"You would, Bart," Kat said.

"Did you see how fast those things move? Catching them is the first thing."

"I caught one," Bart said.

"Luck," Ken said.

"I am a darn good baseball player, Ken. It takes quick reflexes."

Ken shrugged. "Maybe. But I don't think we should depend on your skills at catching a round orb to translate to catching an armed, nasty legendary creature."

"Stop it, you two! This is serious. We need a plan," Kat said.

"I'm going back for Shank. That's my plan," Jet said.

"So you keep saying," Chloe replied.

Bart pointed to the large, round clear disc in the corner. "How powerful is it at picking up sound?"

"The parabolic listening device?" Chloe asked.

"Yeah."

"It picks up sound up to 300 feet away. It has an eight times more sensitive microphone than other listening devices."

"So, it could help alert us to those THINGS?"

"Possible," Chloe said.

"We add it to our arsenal. Just in case," Ken said.

"Alright. Let's make a list of things to take along. Food, water, and microphone on steroids. Anything else?" Bart asked.

"I suggest a Bible and some Holy Water," Ken said.

"Okie Dokie. I've got a Bible. Where do we find Holy Water?" Kat asked.

"Search me," Ken said.

"I suppose I could call Mom. If I have to." Chloe shook her head. "If she gets wind of what we are doing, she's gonna make this trip so much more complicated."

"Do you know anyone else we could call?" Kat asked.

Chloe stared out the window, taking in the fading orange and purple of the sunset. "No."

"Do you *really* think we need Holy Water? Are you guys into voodoo or something?" Jet asked.

"Nope. But the Catholics are big on it. They use it when fighting demons. They've been fighting demons for a couple of thousand years. So, why not use a tried and possibly true method?" Ken said.

"Mom is acquainted, if not friends with, everyone in Hayden. She can tell us," Chloe said. "Maybe she won't ask too many questions—one can always hope."

"Fine, if you call Aunt Rose, Chloe, we will gather what we need and be on the road again before Jet goes off by himself and gets into trouble he won't be able to talk or fight his way out of," Kat said.

"We need a couple of hours of sleep before heading off again," Ken said.

"Agreed."

"You guys get some shut-eye. I'll be back." Jet walked out the door.

Chloe ran after him. "Where are you going?"

"I'm going home to grab a couple of things. In case we need them."

Chloe touched his arm. "Stay and rest. We can all go with you for whatever you need before we leave. Please don't go up there by yourself, Jet. This is not the time to be a lone wolf. Please."

Jet looked at Chloe. He almost jumped backward when he saw the genuine concern in her eyes. No one looked at him that way. He shook the emotions from his head.

"Don't worry, I'll be back. As if I'd let you do this without me. Be ready to go when I get here, or I will go alone."

Chloe smiled. "We will be ready. And, we will find Shank."

"Or I'll die trying." Jet turned and jogged down the street.

CHAPTER 18

"And here we are again," Bart stared at the entrance to Andalusia Forest. He could see the top of the fairy statues' heads several feet in. It sent a chill up his back.

Kat walked up beside him, tippytoed, and stared at the sculptures. "I think those are the evilest-looking sprites I've ever seen," she commented.

"Sure are. It's like the guy who built this place was on a first-name basis with those evil little creatures we ran into," Bart said.

"You think?" Ken asked.

"We need to do some more research on Torrens. Something doesn't add up. This seems more than cursed land," Bart said.

"Darci will do it, and even though she can't be here, she is itching to find out what is happening. She is out of the hospital and still weak but can research. She'll call me if she finds anything."

"Works for me."

A different park warden greeted the team. "You guys sure have friends in high places. And, you must be gluttons for punishment. Didn't your partner have some serious injuries here?"

"Yes. But she is on the mend. Since this is the last place my friend was seen, we need to find out where he might have gone after this," Jet answered.

Wow. The boy can be smooth when he wants to, Ken thought.

The ranger gave a quick nod. "Well, I hope you know what you're doing. Are you sure you want to stay overnight?"

"We think it's important."

"Ok. Here's my number. Call anytime. Otherwise, I'll be back tomorrow."

Jet took the card. "Thanks."

Bart leaned on the gate. Again, it creaked in protest, stuck, and gave way when Bart leaned in harder.

Bart bowed low and waved his arm for the others to enter.

"Wait!" Chloe said. "Who has the parabolic dish?"

"What are you blind, Pip Squeak? I have it right here." Ken patted the shoulder strap and turned to show the large saucer to Chloe.

Chloe let out her breath. "Good. I have the Bible, and Mom got me some Holy Water. Which, by the way, took major explanation to keep her from coming along."

"I bet," Ken said.

Chloe's phone chirped. "Speak of . . . Hi, Mom. No, I'm hiking with Ken and Kat, like I mentioned."

Ken motioned for the phone. Chloe turned it over to him.

"Hi, Aunt Rose. We are getting ready to do an overnight. I promise I'll take good care of Chloe."

"You better, Kenneth. Your neck is on the line if even one hair on her head is touched," Rose said.

"Yes, ma'am. I understand. One of us will call as soon as we are back in town. Bye." Ken hung up before Rose could give any more instructions.

"Overprotective," Chloe said.

"She loves you. And don't you forget it," Ken said.

"Whatever. Let's get going." Chloe walked forward.

The witch house greeted them. "Menacing as it was before," Chloe said.

"If it could be more menacing, I'd say it is," Kat quipped.

"Let's keep walking. I want to make the outbuilding as soon as we can. It's a good place to store our equipment and supplies," Ken said.

"Agree with you, Brother." Bart moved up the path. He stopped short in his tracks. "What is this?" He bent over.

Long streaks of red, followed by drag marks, marked the trail.

"Looks like blood," Ken said.

"Yeah, and those drag marks look like they were made by a human," Bart replied.

"They go off in that direction." Kat pointed up the dirt walk toward a tangled copse of trees and undergrowth.

"You stay here," Ken said to Kat, Chloe, and Jet.

"I'm going with you," Jet said.

"No. You are not."

Jet started up the narrow strip of land.

Bart seized his arm. "You aren't going."

"Stop me." Jet jerked free and started up the road again.

Bart exhaled, laid hold of Jet's right arm, yanked it behind his back, and pulled upward. "You are staying here," Bart growled in his ear.

Chloe ran up to them. "Let him go! You're hurting him."

Bart loosened his grip.

Jet stayed put, anger darkening his chocolate-colored eyes.

"Stop squirming and listen. Ken and I need to follow those tracks. Kat and Chloe need someone here with them. You will do no good for us if you are throwing up over, God forbid, the corpse of your former friend."

"I can take it," Jet said.

"Have you ever seen a dead body?" Ken asked.

"No. But I can take it."

"Maybe. Maybe not. Do you think this is the time to find out? Or do you think you MIGHT be of more help here protecting Kat and Chloe?"

"Please stay, Jet. I'd feel better with you around," Chloe said.

Jet looked from Chloe to Bart. He relaxed.

"That's better. Now stay here. We will be back as soon as possible."

"Fine. If you aren't back in an hour, I'm coming after you," Jet said.

"I am, too," Kat said.

Ken gave a quick nod.

Bart and Ken advanced up the lane, scouring the ground as they went to find clues until they disappeared into the undergrowth.

"I don't feel good about this," Chloe said.

"Neither do I, Chloe. Neither do I."

CHAPTER 19

Ken flipped open a walking stick.

Bart glanced from the cane to Ken. "Tell me."

"Well, after our last foray through the woods, I keep one on hand. Brought it with me from Alaska. When we're not chasing life-threatening entities, Kat and I do enjoy a good hike."

Bart surveyed the landscape. "True. Glad you brought it along. It doesn't happen to have one of those knives in the tip, does it?"

"No. I didn't realize we were going into the jungle." Ken looked around. Tall, razor-thin grasses grew up around the gnarled trunks of oaks and elms. A dark green ivy snaked up the trees, looking like serpents. He shook his head.

"Good thing there isn't any worse vegetation here." Bart walked forward and picked his way through the high growth.

Ken walked ahead of Bart and stopped short when a small deer darted in front of him and to the left, swallowed by the thick greenery.

Spring birds were calling loudly. Ken heard a Robin's mating call and listened as a Mocking Bird mimicked the Robin, a Blue Jay, and then a Cardinal. *It's hard to believe I once didn't think there was an Intelligent Creator of this world and universe.*

Bart caught up and pointed ahead. "Looks like an open field."

Ken nodded and continued forward.

They reached the clearing.

Deep drag marks, blood mixed in, led to a tripod. The tripod stood in the middle of the meadow. Something shiny caught Bart's attention. He walked closer. Hanging from the tripod was a sea-blue piece of glass with a brown object in the middle. Bart reached for the chain. "Ouch!"

Ken turned to Bart. A large drop of blood appeared on his hand, then a blister. Another drop of blood oozed to the skin's surface.

"Back to the trees!" Ken commanded.

Bart and Ken raced toward the woods. The feeling of a hundred pin-pricks hit Ken between the shoulders. He reached into his pocket, pulled out two bottles of liquid, and threw one to Bart.

Bart stopped short and turned. He threw the Holy Water in a semi-circle around him.

Ethereal screams preceded a slight spark, then smoke. Something fell to the earth.

Ken followed Bart's lead.

The same anomaly occurred: Shrieks, sparks, smoke.

"Huh."

The biting stopped. The sound of buzzing insects and wisps of wind rushed past Ken toward the meadow.

Bart crouched down and picked up a dark speck. "Look at this."

Ken bent down. "Another fairy."

"Well, it appears they can be killed."

"I'm developing much more respect for Holy Water," Ken said.

"Let's get out of here."

They raced toward the walkway.

Ken stopped and turned. "We need to find out what is in that patch of grass. Why were those—creatures—protecting it?"

The sound of tiny wings grew louder as Ken advanced.

Bart yanked on his arm. "Not now. Run!"

CHAPTER 20

"I don't know about you two, but I can't stand here watching and praying for someone to return and not do something," Kat said.

"Whatcha got in mind?" Jet asked.

"The Witch House sure put off some weird feelings yesterday," Chloe said.

Jet thought back on the two dolls in the cage. Fear gripped his heart. "Yeah, well, we've been there. Let's go somewhere else."

Chloe lifted an eyebrow. "Is the great Jet afraid of something?"

Anger smoldered in Jet's dark eyes. "I'm not afraid of anything. We've been there. That's all."

"Well, we found Shank's knife close by, right? So, there may be more clues about what happened to Shank in the hut. We didn't get a chance to finish exploring it."

"Chloe's right. Let's go." Kat took off toward the moss-covered hat towering just above the tree line.

"Fine," Jet said.

Kat took in the faded mural in the main room. A small boy and girl surrounded by candy cane trees and gumdrop flowers skipped up a chocolate-brick candy walk to a gingerbread house. White icing and a gumdrop roof topped the one-story cabin.

Kat looked at the second mural. The same children stood on the gingerbread porch of the house.

The following picture depicted a sweet-looking, grandmotherly figure holding a plate of fresh baked goods, inviting the children to eat.

"This is the most sinister children's attraction I've ever seen," Kat said.

"That's what I said yesterday," Chloe answered.

"Let's just shut up and start looking." Jet walked into the room where the caged dolls were exhibited.

Chloe followed him.

Kat scoured the floor on the way to the room. She knelt when her flashlight caught an anomaly in the dust-covered boards on the floor. "Are these Shank's?"

"What?" Jet asked.

Kat held out a pack of *Marlboro* cigarettes and a silver lighter decorated with skull and crossbones.

Jet grabbed them. "Yes! That's his lighter, and this is what he smokes."

"Okay. We know Shank was here. Now where did he go after this?" Kat asked.

Chloe studied the floor. "Guys. . ."

Kat crouched down, balancing on the balls of her feet, and read, "Lucius owns this land. Be warned. If you are here, Lucius owns you, too. Prepare to meet your destiny."

"Who is Lucius?" Jet asked.

Kat stood. "Or what is a Lucius? In my experience, these types of warnings aren't about a human. So, it begs the question, what?"

"Probably some kids got in here and tried to scare us. That's all," Jet said.

Chloe whirled 180 degrees toward a sharp *crack* of wood. Her flashlight caught a black, hair-covered claw as it disappeared into the wall. "What was that?"

"What was what?" Jet asked. "This place is getting to you now, isn't it?"

"I saw a large claw—like a spider's leg but HUGE."

Kat walked to the wall. She ran her hand over the area. "There's nothing here now."

They explored the rest of the witch's hut.

"Let's head back," Chloe said.

The hair on Kat's neck came to attention. She turned and faced the cage and dolls.

Two sets of glowing yellow eyes greeted her. The two mouths seemed to have widened into a large, toothy grin. Kat felt ire instead of fear. "Hey.

Ghost. Creep. Have you got nothing better than animated dolls?" She shouted into the dark room.

Jet and Chloe came up beside Kat.

Chloe's eyes widened. She took a step backward.

"I told you," Jet whispered.

Chloe clenched Jet's forearm. The feel of his arm beneath the jacket gave her a sense of calm. "I believe you now."

Kat strolled toward the cage.

Jet took hold of her arm and pulled Kat backward.

She shook free, continued forward, and shouted, "If that's all you got, I laugh at you. I've been chased by an alligator man, been harassed by demons, and even died, for a while, once. You'll have to try harder to scare this woman." She shook the cage doors. "Do you hear me?"

The whole house creaked, then vibrated.

Kat released the cage bars, stood stock-still, and searched the room with her eyes.

A large shadow appeared on the left wall of the mural room. A high-pitched screech permeated the witch's house. The floor shook in rhythm to heavy boots advancing from the mural room to the doll cage room.

"Well, this is just great," Chloe said. "Did you have to challenge whatever is here? *Did you?*"

Kat whirled toward the door. "In the name of Jesus, STOP."

The shaking, shuddering, and convulsing of the building ceased. A menacing hush fell over the house. *Like the calm before the great wind of a storm,* Kat thought. She stiffened.

"In the name of Jesus, tell me who you are." Kat could not believe the strength in her words. *I sound like Grandma Bricken; worse, I sound like Josiah Williams.* Kat thought about her grandmother and Josiah, who had helped her through so much in the past. *Wish you were here.*

"I am Bête Noire," a disembodied voice replied.

"Who are you?"

"I am the keeper of this portal. I am what your nightmares are made of. I AM your nightmare." The thing ran forward, heavy boots clomping toward Kat.

Kat grabbed her arm and screamed. She clutched her other arm. Chloe ran forward and snatched hold of Kat's shirt, pulling Kat backward until she was out of the thing's reach.

The dolls in the cage started laughing, then spitting at the trio. "You will be our dinner," the dolls said in unison. They clapped long-rotted away hands. The small cage door squeaked and moved to the open position. The dolls jumped out and staggered toward the trio, pieces of straw dropping from the rotted fabric of their legs.

"I'll be a monkey's uncle if you're going to eat any of us," Kat said. "I am not afraid of you. Nor will I be your fodder. I've been up against much worse, and it couldn't take me out. You know why? Because God fights my battles, that's why!"

Kat fell to her knees as the dolls advanced on one side and the entity on the other.

Sinister laughs bombarded her ears as they closed in.

"Down. Now." Kat commanded Jet and Chloe.

Without an argument, her two pale-faced companions dropped to their knees.

"O God, please help us. I cannot fight this battle without You. It is a spiritual battle. Send Your holy angel, O God. Fight for us! In Your Son Jesus' mighty name." Kat held her breath and the hands of Chloe and Jet.

Kat smelled the putrid, sulfur breath of the demon, Bête Noire. She squeezed her eyes shut and waited. If God chose to intervene, He would. If not, she knew she was going home to heaven. *Either way, I win.*

The malicious cackling laughter turned to shrieks of fear and horror in the twinkling of an eye.

Kat's eyelids flew open. A familiar blue light filled the dank, dark cottage. She thought she smelled ions right before the storm-clouded skies opened up and drenched the earth. She lifted her head. She looked at Chloe and Jet.

Chloe turned saucer eyes to Kat; Jet's eyes were glazed, reminiscent of a small animal caught in a car's headlights.

"Thank you, God!" Kat jumped to her feet.

An angel floated to the ground in front of her and the others.

"Bête Noire," the angel said. "I am Raphael, sent by the Almighty God." Raphael thrust his sword outward and cut through the black entity. It shriveled and disappeared in a cloud of smoke. "Be gone, you two minions of evil, never to haunt this place again." Raphael swung the sword, and the two dolls were cut in two. The yellow light and snarling smiles disappeared. Only black dots where the yellow eyes had been and a mouth remained.

Kat fell to her knees again. "Thank you," she whispered to Raphael.

Raphael lowered his sword. "Do not kneel before me. I am a servant of the Most High, as are you. Stand and give glory to Him alone!"

Kat stood up, hoping her shaking legs would hold her. "Right!"

"Thank you, O God. Thank you, Jesus," she prayed.

Raphael gave an almost invisible smile and soared up through the roof. The blue light dissipated, leaving Chloe, Jet, and Kat in the dark once again.

"Ummm, what did I just see?" Jet whispered.

"Well, as if you didn't know—an angel," Chloe said.

"Right. And angels come at your command?" He asked Kat.

"No. But God saw fit for you two to see His power first-hand. I suggest you ruminate on it. We are not in a human battle. We are in a spiritual battle. Remember that!"

She marched to the door of the witch's house, then turned. "You two coming, or are you going to sit here all day? We have work to do."

Kat surveyed the gravel pathway, expecting Ken and Bart to be there and reprimand them for leaving.

"Why aren't Ken and Bart here?" Chloe asked Kat's unspoken question.

"This isn't good. They are an hour overdue," Jet said.

A loud noise, almost a scream, shattered the park's quiet.

"They're in trouble." Kat took off running.

"Hey, wait up!" Jet took off after her, and Chloe ran a close third as they made their way to the thick woods.

CHAPTER 21

Kat stood back and peered into the undergrowth. "Nothing." She strode closer to the thick foliage.

Jet put a hand on Kat's arm. "Not a good idea. We don't need to all get lost in there."

"They've been almost two hours. Why aren't they back?" Kat asked.

"I'm not sure, but I think after the scream, it is time for us to call in some help," Chloe said.

"Right."

Chloe dialed the Ranger's phone number, then lowered her phone when she saw Ken and Bart running toward her and Kat.

"Where have you two been? It's been almost two hours! I was calling the Ranger to bring the police."

"It can't have been two hours. We just left." Bart looked at his watch.

Kat shoved her phone in Bart's face. "You left two hours ago."

"That's not possible."

Ken looked at Kat's phone and then at his watch. "I'll be. My watch stopped 20 minutes after we left."

"Do you believe me now?"

"I do," Ken said. He shook his head.

"Well, where were you?" Jet asked.

"We followed the tracks to an open field. Weird place. There was a tripod-type thing in the middle with something hanging from it. I went to take a look. And . . ."

"And that's when we were attacked," Bart said.

"Attacked? By what?" Chloe asked.

"Same creatures who attacked Darci," Ken mumbled.

"Excuse me? Did you mean fairies?" Kat asked.

Ken nodded. He pulled his shirt down in the back so Kat could assess the injuries.

"Bart has the same. They are nasty creatures."

"How did you get away?"

"It may sound weird, but Holy Water," Bart replied.

Jet snorted. "Sure it was."

"Believe what you will, but that's what happened." Bart took a handkerchief from his pocket and opened it. Inside was a tiny, soot-covered body. The wings, although singed, were still visible.

Kat, Chloe, and Jet gathered around.

"Those are definitely the same—beings—who attacked Darci. I thought I was imagining things," Chloe said.

"These pixies are protecting something in the open field. And, they are vicious about it," Bart said.

"I wonder what's so important," Chloe said.

"What they're protecting isn't important. Did you find Shank?" Jet asked.

"Not yet. But the drag marks went straight into the open field and stopped at the tripod. Whatever made those tracks, well, it doesn't look good," Bart said.

"I'm not giving up on Shank. You guys can if you want, but I will find him." Jet retrieved his backpack and started up the pathway. "He's got to be somewhere. I'm going to the clearing myself."

Chloe touched Jet's black leather jacket. "Wait. We need to find out what we are up against first. You saw what just happened."

"What happened?" Ken scowled at Kat. "Didn't you stay on the dirt path?"

Kat's stormy emerald-green eyes met Ken's. "We explored the witch's hut."

Red crept from Ken's collar to his face. "Why?" He growled.

Chloe stepped between Kat and Ken. "We agreed to go. We thought we could find more clues to lead us to Shank."

"We couldn't stand here like pudding heads," Kat said.

"Did you find anything?" Ken asked.

"Well, yes, we did." Chloe held out the cigarettes and lighter. "These are Shank's."

"All those items tell us is he was there. Not where he is," Bart said.

"We had one crazy thing happen while we were there. Your woman is quite the warrior," Jet said.

Ken's eyes widened. "Crazy thing? What crazy thing, Kat?"

"The normal. Demons, prayer, angel rescued us. You know, the normal."

"I can't leave you unsupervised for a second, can I, Cous?" Bart asked.

"She handled it. Let it go," Chloe said in Kat's defense.

"We have other fish to fry," Kat said.

"What's more important than your safety?" Ken said.

"All of our safety," Kat quipped. "We found a message in the hut. Talked about a Lucius. Said anyone on this land is now his property. Does anyone here know about a guy named Lucius?" Kat asked.

Jet shrugged.

Ken shook his head.

"I'll ask Darci to do some digging." Chloe pulled the phone from her pocket and dialed.

"Ask if she's come across something like the weird necklace we saw hanging in the meadow while you are at it," Bart said.

"Will do."

CHAPTER 22

Lucius stood beside the aquamarine pool, encircled by small, flying humanoids. A hundred of them wore red caps. The blue sprites who had attacked Bart and Ken made up the remainder of the gathering.

"It's about time you arrived," Lucius told the Red Caps.

"We had other things to do. Why did you summon us?" Burkist, the leader asked.

"Aren't you hungry?" Lucius asked.

"We are always hungry." Burkist snatched a blue fairy and tore into its flesh. A small spurt of red blood came from the fairy before it went limp. He swallowed it and swiped at another.

"ENOUGH! You are not to eat any more of your kind. You have a bigger prize here— humans."

Burkist released the pixie. "What humans?"

"There are several who have invaded my domain. I want all of them exterminated."

"What's so important about these mortals? You've never called us in before. You took care of it yourself."

"These are strong in The One."

Burkist glided to the forest's edge, his army with him.

The buzz of Red Cap conversation rose throughout the meadow, sounding like a thousand angry gnats.

Burkist faced Lucius. "Why would I risk my life, not to mention my army's lives, for you?"

"Afraid? I thought Red Caps had no fear," Lucius mocked.

"You say afraid. I say prudent. The One has all power. I'm not looking forward to eternal damnation earlier than it must be."

"If we win this battle, there is no eternal damnation. Well, not until a much, much later time."

"Why?"

Lucius pointed to the pendant hanging on the tripod. "As long that remains suspended, no human power can touch me. As long as I am untouchable, I will continue to implement the decision of our master, to destroy mankind. The bobble is your insurance, too."

Burkist soared to the tripod and examined the object in the middle. He looked below. "Who is this?"

"Oh, just a wanderer. As a good-faith effort, you can have him first if you'd like."

Burkist's mouth watered as he stared into terrified eyes. "Oh, I'd like that very much. Alright. It will be done. Now, my fellows, we feast."

"Wait. Tie the human's mouth first. We can't have the others hear him."

Burkist ripped a large piece of fabric from Shank's shirt. "So be it." He stuffed the cloth into Shank's mouth and took a bite of his cheek. "Perfect. Not too young; not too old." He sunk his teeth into Shank's left eye.

The army descended.

The muffled screams grew fewer until Shank stood silent.

"This is what happens to anyone who tries to take my prize. You will remember this forever, won't you human?" Lucius said.

Lucius laughed when the Red Caps dipped their hats in Shank's blood and put them back on their heads.

CHAPTER 23

Ken hoisted his pack. "Let's head to the office we found yesterday. It's the only place no one has had a bad experience."

"Right." Bart picked up his pack and looked at the others. "You coming?"

"Right behind you," Kat said.

Ken opened the plank-wood door and threw his pack on the ground. "Okay. So, what is our next plan of action?"

"Hey, Darci just called," Chloe said.

"And?" Bart asked.

"And, she researched the name Lucius."

"I didn't expect to hear from Darci today," Kat said.

"She is one efficient person. And she is bored beyond belief. Anyway, she said there is a legend about a guy named Lucius. He appears to people in desperate need of something—healing, at the point of bankruptcy, and more."

"Okay. What's this Lucius got to do with this place?" Ken asked

"It's reported Roy Torrens talked about meeting a guy named Lucius right before he started Andalusia Forest. His daughter was in a wheelchair. He despaired over it to anyone who would listen. Got in some fights because she was being bullied. He met this Lucius guy, and his whole attitude changed. He went from being angry and depressed to being happy—overnight."

"Did anyone say why?" Kat asked

"Yeah. Torrens told a local bartender his daughter would be healed and live for a long, long time. Before that, all he talked about was how she would die soon, and he would kill himself if she did."

"This Lucius character cured her?" Bart asked

"That's the story. Lucius is a mysterious person who shows up and performs miracles. Several townspeople talk about it. Some of them say he is Jesus in the flesh."

"That's stretching it since the Bible's pretty specific about Jesus. He's going to come back on the clouds," Ken said.

"What are you talking about?" Jet asked. "You mean you believe in Jesus? And he is going to return to Earth? Why? If I got out of here, I'd stay out."

"I'm thankful to say you aren't He," Kat quipped.

"So, I'd say we have a false prophet here. What do you say, Ken?" Kat asked.

"I'd say. And, I've seen enough to believe there are many with false hopes in evil entities who pretend they are here to do good."

"I remember Mom warning me! She'd always quote something from her Bible in hopes I wouldn't get involved with the wrong people as I was growing up, '. . . for Satan himself masquerades as an angel of light. It is not surprising, then, if his servants masquerade as servants of righteousness.'"

"Second Corinthians 11:14," Kat whispered.

"Yep. That's it, alright," Chloe said. "It's the only verse I've memorized. Mom said it over and over and over—you have the idea."

"Did it work?"

"Well. I'm not going around with some crazy guy," Chloe laughed. "Unless you count Jet."

"Hey! I'm not crazy. I'm my own individual."

"Back to the topic at hand," Bart said.

"Right. This Lucius legend has been in the area for hundreds of years. The thing is, people's wishes are granted, but it never ends well."

"Like all the rumors of deaths around this place?" Kat asked.

"Yeah. Even Torrens himself came to a nasty end. Legend has it Torrens jumped from those falls in an attempted suicide. He lived for a few days, though, in lots of pain. He said something about his little girl would live forever, but he kept saying she was a monster and then talked about other crazy things like demons and fairies. His final days were tortuous."

"Maybe his ramblings weren't so crazy," Kat said.

"What about the necklace we saw?" Bart asked.

"She came across one small article about an amulet, which sounds like what you saw. She said there is an artifact which had been on the underground circuit around the 1940s and 1950s. It was said to be ancient. Like 2,000 years ancient."

"What made this so special?" Ken asked.

"The rumor is it is a thorn from the Crown of Thorns."

"You mean the crown of thorns on Jesus' head at the crucifixion?"

"Yep."

"It was wood. It couldn't survive this long," Kat said.

"Well, that's where it got interesting. It was encased in glass from the Roman Empire era. The glass could have survived this long."

"What happened to it?" Ken asked.

"No one can say. It disappeared in the 1950s, and no one has seen it since."

"You think Torrens had it?"

"It's possible. And, from what the article said, this artifact didn't stay in one person's possession for long."

"Why not?"

"People said it was a bad luck charm," Chloe said.

"If it is a thorn from the crown, wouldn't it be a good luck piece?"

"I didn't say it's logical. It's what the article said. It said anyone who owned it would start seeing visions. They would be convicted of anything they weren't doing right."

"Like Paul on the road to Damascus?"

"Kind of. And, it brought many of them to the brink of insanity."

"Wow. I sure don't want to be told everything I've done wrong in my life," Jet said.

"I wouldn't want to be you and faced with your past," Chloe said.

"Very funny. And, since this is hogwash, I think we should forget about it and try and find Shank."

"That's the plan," Ken said.

Kat pointed at the window. "Something is outside."

A small, winged humanoid with a red cap sat on the exterior windowsill.

Ken strode to the window and tapped. "Get out of here!"

The creature opened its mouth in a wide snarl and rammed its body against the window. The glass shook.

"Holy Moly, that's one strong insect," Jet said.

Bart bent closer to the window. "It's another fairy, I think. Look at those wings."

"Why is it wearing a red cap? The blue creatures didn't wear any caps," Kat said.

"Not to mention it's bigger than the others and uglier," Chloe said.

"I saw something about a red-capped creature in Darci's notebook. Hold on." Chloe pulled the notebook from her backpack.

"Here it is: 'Red Caps also originated in Scotland.'"

"Scotland is not the place to be, in my opinion," Kat interjected.

Chloe continued, "They were like minuscule Jason Voorhees of the fairy world—murderous and unstoppable. Although depicted as gaunt old men, Red Caps were armed with sharp claws and teeth. They had super strength and could overpower a grown man. As if their power wasn't scary enough, they also carried around a scythe, which they used to hack and slash people to death. After they murdered their victims, the Red Cap would mop up the blood with its hat, hence the name. These fays were also alleged to be cannibals who ate both humans and other fairies. Reciting biblical verses was the only way to ward off these murderous critters. The victim had to be pretty quick because not only were Red Caps strong, they were also swift."

"Oh, this is not sounding good," Bart said.

Chloe looked at the windowsill. "It's not looking good at all."

Several red-capped creatures lined the windowsill. Their red caps glistened in the sunlight.

"Ummm. Is it me, or do those guys have blood on their hats?" Kat asked.

"It's not just you. I think that's what it is. And it's fresh," Bart said.

Kat heard the unmistakable *clink* of metal on glass. She squinted and backed to the far corner of the room. "Are they holding curved knives?"

"Yes. I think they are," Chloe said.

"It's safe to assume they aren't friendly," Jet quipped.

"Yes, Jet, I do think they mean us harm," Bart said.

"Just once, I'd like to meet a friendly supernatural entity," Ken lamented.

Bart sighed. "It's time to do battle, my friends. Buckle up."

Chloe ripped the Bible from her backpack. "What are we supposed to read?"

"Good question," Ken said.

"Well, I don't know *What* you're supposed to read, but you better read something quick!" Jet pointed at the window.

The fairies stood shoulder to shoulder. They hacked at the window glass with the scythes. The once unblemished pane was now full of star breaks.

The sound of hundreds of tiny bullets came from the wood entrance.

Kat ran to the door. "Find something to hold this thing," she shouted over her shoulder.

Ken rushed over to a roughhewn bench. "Grab the other end, Bart."

"Ooomph," Bart exclaimed.

"Move over, Old Man," Jet yanked on the end of the bench and strained to lift it. "What did they do, build it to withstand a tornado?"

"Old man, huh?" Bart took hold of the middle.

They guided it to the door, barricading the entrance, just as a small hole appeared.

"Just in time," Chloe said.

"Or not!" Kat eyed the window.

One of the six panes of glass shattered. The sallow-skinned beings shimmied through the opening, ignoring the jagged glass as it cut their clothing.

Chloe let the Bible fall open. It landed on Psalm 5. She stared at the words.

The Red Caps poured through the window like salt from a pitcher.

"Go for the men first," Burkist bellowed.

The winged entities started toward Ken, Bart, and Jet, some flying, others marching.

Jet managed to slap one of them.

It sailed backward, hitting the old radio equipment. "Ahhhh!" The Red Cap shook itself and raced forward, pulling the scythe from behind its back, aiming it at Jet's forehead.

"Chloe, READ," Kat screamed.

"Give ear to my words, O Lord, consider my sighing. Listen to my cry for help, my King and my God, for to You I pray," Chloe read.

The Red Caps fell to the ground like large raindrops during a storm.

Burkist, bleeding from his nose, screamed, "RETREAT," in a shrill voice that reminded Kat of Alvin the Chipmunk.

Hundreds of the hand-sized warriors yowled, then bolted for the window, hands over their ears.

Chloe held the bible waist high and stared at the Red Caps crawling through the window.

Burkist reeled away from the hole and winged toward Bart, scythe pulled.

"Keep reading, Chloe," Kat yelled.

"You are not a God who takes pleasure in evil; with You, the wicked cannot dwell. The arrogant cannot stand in Your presence." Chloe's voice had grown stronger and louder with each word.

"In the name of Jesus, BE gone," Ken shouted.

"Amen," Bart answered.

Burkist tumbled backward through the air, hitting the wall beside the window before crawling across the wooden plank and out the broken glass. Once outside, he turned, blood still streaming from his bulbous nose.

"We are not done here! You will be sorry you ever messed with my troops."

"…You hate all who do wrong . . ." Chloe continued.

The leader shrieked, covered his ears, and rushed to the tree line.

"Wow," Kat said, never turning her eyes away from the window and the fleeing nymphs beyond.

"Okay. Is anyone hurt?" Bart asked.

The spell over the rest of them broke.

Kat studied the others. "I'm not sure how, but we are unscathed. It is a miracle. Thank you, Jesus," she whispered.

"This is not the safest place to be," Bart said.

"What was your first clue, Old Man?" Jet asked.

"You call me Old Man one more time, I'll show you what I can do to your young, arrogant face," Bart threatened.

Jet opened his mouth to retort.

Bart stepped forward.

Jet clamped his jaw and turned to Chloe. "Great reading, Chloe-girl. Didn't know you could shout so loud."

"I didn't shout."

"You did," Kat said with a smile. "You were on fire."

"Fear will do that for me," Chloe answered.

"Where do you suggest we go? We need to find a place to call base camp before looking for Shank."

"The house may be our best bet," Ken said.

"Are you kidding me? Weren't you with me when we were attacked by some odd, and may I say, rage-filled spirit-woman? Or maybe you forgot about those other fairies?" Bart said.

"It is the most solid structure we've seen here. It has various rooms in which to barricade ourselves, so if any of you have a better idea, now is the time to speak up," Ken replied.

The silence was so loud in the room a pin dropping would have sounded like a nuclear explosion.

"Anyone?" Ken asked. "No? Then let's make our way to the house before dark."

The three men dragged the rough and heavy bench toward the middle of the room.

Ken strode to the door.

Chloe threw the backpack over her shoulder and clenched the Bible in her right hand like a lifeline for a drowning person.

Kat eyed Chloe's white knuckles around the Bible. She put a hand over Chloe's. "You did great, Chloe. I can't tell you to relax, but I can tell you God knows what will happen. So, relax as best you can. He's got us."

"Well, it's not like I don't believe in God," Chloe said. "I don't understand what He's going to do, so I think I'll keep on keeping on until He clues me in."

"You are doing great."

"I thought ghost hunting was a great idea. I always wanted to understand what was on the other side. I'm not sure I was ready for what we've found here."

"Well, I'm no preacher," Kat said. "In fact, not long ago, I didn't believe there was a God. But I'm here to tell you I know there is. And I had to see some unimaginable things to believe. So, just be willing to believe God is here, and He loves you. That's where to start."

Chloe nodded. "I'll try."

"And, I suggest you go up and talk to Jet. He looks like he could use a friend."

"He's such a baby," Chloe said.

Kat laughed. "Yeah, we are all babies at one time or another."

CHAPTER 24

Jet stomped, more than walked, toward the haunted house.

Chloe swept up beside him.

"What do you want? To tell me how wimpy I am? I don't need you to tell me."

"I don't think you are wimpy, Jet," Chloe said softly.

Jet looked at Chloe. He took in her red hair and buff-colored skin, dashed with freckles. The freckles reminded him of cinnamon floating on cream. *She is beautiful in her own unique way*, he thought.

Chloe looked into Jet's dark eyes. "Do I have something on my face?"

"No."

"Why are you staring."

"I'm not."

"Yes, you are."

"Whatever." Jet walked faster to escape the awkward conversation.

Chloe stood still for a moment, then ran to catch up with him.

"I was thinking. When, or if, we get out of here, do you want to go to a movie or something?" Jet asked.

Chloe planted her feet, gripping Jet's upper arm. "What did you say?"

"I didn't stutter."

Chloe searched Jet's eyes. He looked serious. Chloe's stomach started to churn, and her heart quickened. *Stop it, Chloe. He is not your type.*

"Yeah, right. Good joke," Chloe took off up the trail at a fast clip.

"What lit a fire under her?" Kat asked.

Jet shrugged. "I haven't a clue. I don't understand you women at all." Jet took off after Chloe.

Kat smiled.

"Why do you look like the Cheshire Cat?" Ken asked.

"I think love is in the air."

Ken looked after Chloe. "Oh, I hope not with that smart-mouthed kid."

"I think it is with that smart-mouthed kid."

"No accounting for taste," Ken said.

"You should know, FBI," Kat remembered her instant dislike of Ken at their first meeting. If someone had told her Ken was the man she would marry, she would have laughed—and hard. But her grandmother knew. And, per usual, Grandma Bricken was right.

"I wasn't a delinquent," Ken said.

"No. You were an arrogant know-it-all from the big city. And, look, you changed." Kat snickered and started up the trail.

"Not the same thing."

"These are the ones who defeated Iconoclast," Evikal said. He referenced the great Commander of the evil foe, the one who had been undefeated until he fought—on several occasions—a small clan of warriors from Ravens Cove, Alaska. They defeated him in Bordman's Crossing, only miles from Torrens Falls.

"He was weak," Perse said.

"He is one of Satan's greatest commanders."

"Not anymore. Now he's something else." Perse smiled because he had always hated Iconoclast. "Lucius will not be defeated, which means we won't."

A bellow which sounded like a Stag deer in pain, reached their ears.

"Something has happened. We must return to the clearing."

CHAPTER 25

Kat, Bart, Ken, Chloe, and Jet reached the old haunted house. The sun glinted above the trees.

"It doesn't look much better than before," Chloe commented.

"Are we sure we want to hole up here?" Bart said.

"I asked before, and I'll ask again. Does anyone have a better idea? Those red-capped monsters can make their way through anything by the looks of it. This house has enough rooms. We might be able to fortify one," Ken said.

"Thinking," Bart replied.

Chloe's phone rang. "Hello? It's Mom." She mouthed at Ken.

Ken's eyes grew wide. He motioned for Chloe to give him the phone.

"Hold on, Mom. Ken wants to talk to you."

"Kenneth, why did you let Chloe go to that horrid abomination? It's cursed!"

"Ummm, Aunt Rose, how did you find out we are here?"

"I had a vision. I've told you about my visions before. So, God told me. That's how. Leave there now."

We can't, Ma'am." Ken felt like he was again the twelve-year-old boy being scolded for pulling up her prized roses.

"Why not?"

"Well, we are locked in."

"Call the rangers and run as far away as you can!"

"We will."

"Now!"

Chloe took the phone back. "Mom. We are looking for a friend. He's been missing for a few days. His mom needs him, and the police won't help."

Dead silence.

"Mom?"

"I'm here. You can't do this without help. I'm calling Pastor Morton. You are in a place of great evil. Do you understand?"

"No, Mom, I don't. There are some weird things here but great evil? That's pretty harsh."

"And let's call a potato a potato, not a turnip. Have you heard of the legend of Lucius?"

"Kind of," Chloe resisted scuffing her feet along the dirt like a child telling a tale.

"It's not a legend. This Lucius character has been in the area forever. He offers miracles to the hopeless. He grants the miracle but never in a good way. It is said he is the Devil himself. People die horrifying deaths around him. Andalusia Forest has been cursed for decades and continues to be so. So, if you aren't getting out, I'm sending Pastor Morton."

Fear welled up in Chloe. She took a deep breath. "Mom, we are ok."

"I'm sending him, and that's final." The phone line went dead.

Chloe let out a heavy sigh. "So now she's sending her pastor."

"How is he going to get in?"

"Mom knows everybody. He'll get in."

Movement above Chloe's head caught Ken's attention. "Run! Now!" He swooped Chloe into his arms, ran for the porch, and into the haunted mansion.

Kat, Jet, and Bart jogged up the porch steps and into the mansion. Ken slammed the door.

The sound of a thousand small shots struck the door as he leaned on it.

"What is that?" Bart asked.

"I think it's those flying nymphs again. But I'm not sure which ones. I wasn't going to wait to find out."

"Well, seems the decision is made for us. We camp out here until morning. Then, let's find the field with the tripod again," Bart said.

They picked their way up the decaying staircase and found an empty room with no windows.

"This may work best of all," Ken said

Bart pulled out his flashlight and scanned the emptiness. "I'm inclined to agree," Bart said.

"I pray God protects us and no evil can follow us into this room. In Jesus' name," Kat whispered.

"Amen," Ken said.

An ethereal screech echoed through the house. "If I'm not mistaken, that's the lovely ghost who tried to take us out the first time."

"Didn't sound any too happy," Chloe said.

The doorknob rattled, and the door danced in its frame.

Kat stared at the vibrating aperture and held her breath. The wood bent inward and creaked in protest. Nails popped and clanked to the ground. "Maybe not such a good idea," Kat said.

The door bowed further inward, hinges groaning. The door whiplashed backward into place. Silence fell over the room.

Chloe sighed. "Not good."

"Nope. But it stopped. I do believe we will sleep in safety tonight. Thank you, Jesus," Kat said.

CHAPTER 26

"Wow. That's the best night's sleep I've had in ages," Jet said.

"Well, now we need to be on our way," Ken said.

He opened the door and peered up and down the hallway. "Something was busy last night."

A long side table was tipped on its back, chairs were stacked one on top of the other, and the banister looked like someone drove a small truck through it.

"Not a happy busy, either," Kat said.

"Nope," Ken said.

"Man, this ghost has one bad temper," Bart said.

The troupe made their way down the stairs and out into the sunshine.

"So, where's this clearing?"

"It's back up the trail, past the small work hut. I think."

"No time like the present," Ken said.

The morning sun rippled through the trees. The leaves whispered in a light breeze. Kat trembled. *Those whispers don't sound friendly,* she thought.

"How can a place of such beauty have such a threatening feel?" Chloe asked.

"Just what I was thinking," Jet replied.

Chloe gave a quick smile to Jet. "You don't say." She walked off before he could answer.

The group walked in silence, all aware of their surroundings and bracing for the slightest sign of an attack.

"This isn't the way," Ken said.

"You're right. How did we get there?"

They doubled back to the pathway at the entrance.

"Hello." A tall man waved at them from the gate.

"Pastor Morton, I assume," Ken said.

"Indeed."

A voice came from behind the pastor. "Let us in, Kenneth Melbourne."

"Mom?" Chloe said.

"Aunt Rose?" Ken asked.

Rose stepped up to the gate. Her red hair, highlighted by gray, surrounded her face like a lion. "Yes. Let us in."

"Aunt Rose, why are you here?" Ken asked.

"She's one of the strongest prayer warriors I know," Pastor Morton said.

"That's awesome. But my aunt still should go home. You can pray from anywhere—and stay safe," Ken said.

"I will not let my only daughter and the boy I brought up as my son go into the dragon's lair without me."

Kat shook her head. "This stubbornness runs in both our families." She walked up to the gate. "Come on in. The more, the merrier."

"Not funny, Kat," Ken growled. "Not funny at all."

"What? Are you going to leave them standing in the sun all day? They'll get in anyway."

"Yes. They will."

"Oh, hello, Ranger Perez," Aunt Rose said.

"Hello, I can't begin to comprehend why you want to join these crazies in Andalusia Forest, but here you go." Perez opened the gate.

"I will be back tomorrow morning. First light. Oh," Ranger Perez handed over a radio phone. "Take this. I'll be listening all night."

Bart took the phone. "Thank you. Hope we won't need to use it."

"Me, too. I could use some sleep," Ranger Perez said.

"Lead the way, Kenneth," Rose said.

Ken strode up the footpath.

"Ken, slow down. Aunt Rose needs to keep up," Kat said.

"Oh, I'll keep up; and whatever is here had best realize it has met its match," Rose followed at a speed which belied her age.

CHAPTER 27

The group cut through the brush on the edge of the walkway.

"I remember why we couldn't find the meadow. It came up out of nowhere. No paths to it, nothing," Bart said.

"And, here we are," Ken said.

"What is that horrible stench?" Pastor Morton asked.

Kat took a whiff of the air, covered her mouth, and choked. A sickening-sweet stench mixed with blood filled her nose. "It's death."

"Some animal died close by," Chloe said.

Deafening silence invaded the small, grassy field. In the distance, Blue Jays screeched in alarm. No birds or animals made a sound near this meadow. No wildflowers or shrubs grew here. The grass, although present, was more in hues of yellow than green. It looked scorched. The closer the grass was to the pool in the middle, the yellower and browner it became.

Jet took a step toward the tripod. The ground started shaking.

"Stop in the name of Jesus," Pastor Morton said.

The vibrating earth calmed.

A low buzzing sound from the forest grew louder as it approached the glade.

"Are those fairies?" Aunt Rose asked.

"Yes. And not friendly ones, Mom."

"I'm not so friendly at times like these," Rose replied. She stepped forward. "You are abominations of the earth, created from evil souls! Be gone in the name of Jesus!"

The buzzing stopped. It started again.

"Your words can't stop us, Old Woman." Perse charged forward.

"My words are a shield against you," Rose threw up a hand and thrust it forward.

The fairy somersaulted backward, collided with a tree, and righted itself before flying into the dense vegetation.

Chloe looked at her mother and grinned. "Way to go, Mom."

Rose touched Chloe's cheek. "This is not a game. These creatures are powerful. You should never have come here. When I have you safe at home, I'm grounding you until I've gone to heaven!"

Jet walked forward again. "What's in the water below the tripod?" He looked down, recognition dawned, and he turned and threw up.

"Oh, no." Chloe ran to Jet's side.

"It's Shank—or what's left of him."

Ken joined Chloe and Jet. "Poor soul. He didn't stand a chance."

Kat looked down into the small pond. The bloody remains of a human, head suspended above the water by a crude wood collar, eyes pitted as if they'd been pecked out by a bird, stared back at her. The corpse's mouth stood open as if in a perpetual scream. A piece of fabric still hung on the dead man's tongue. Water lapped against the sides of the hole, carrying bits of flesh and clothing in its waves.

Tears popped into Kat's eyes. She turned away.

"I'm going to kill whoever did this to you, Shank, I swear!" Jet leveled his gaze at Chloe. "I'll kill the creep!"

"No, you won't," A red-capped creature growled.

Jet pulled a switchblade from his back pocket. One *click* and a silver blade glinted in the sunlight. He held it in front of him like a miniature sword. He rushed toward the Red Cap.

"This isn't going to end well," Bart said and started after Jet.

A malevolent laugh rippled through the Red Caps gathered at the tree line.

"Oh, I love fresh meat," Burkist said.

"You're the only one who will be fresh meat, you disgusting miniature monster," Jet said.

The sound of the sharp scythe cutting the air met Kat's ears. She ran toward Bart. "Come back! Both of you!" She turned to Chloe. "We need the Bible. Now!"

The Red Caps closed in on Jet and Bart. Terror gripped Kat's stomach when Bart's ear turned blood-red, and large maroon drops fell from his earlobe onto the yellow grass.

"Ouch!" Jet exclaimed when a small scythe sliced his hand. He dropped the switchblade.

Chloe fumbled through her backpack and pulled out the Bible. "Got it."

"Start reading." Kat swatted at the red-capped fairies with her backpack.

Ken grabbed Kat and drew her away from the battle.

"Let me go." Kat shook free and dashed forward.

Ken caught her arm. "Stop. You can't defeat them with this."

"To you, O Lord, I lift up my soul; in You I trust, O my God. Do not let me be put to shame, nor let my enemies triumph over me." Pastor Morton's baritone voice thundered through the air.

The sound of clanging metal stopped.

Red Caps screamed, some dropping to the ground, others flying into the trees.

"This is for Shank!" Jet screamed and stomped on a Red Cap. He raised his foot again, planted it on the being, and twisted. "You evil, good for nothing. . . thing!"

Bart gripped Jet's elbow. "Come on; it's dead."

Jet's breathing calmed, and he looked at the thing. "It better be."

Kat ran up to Bart. "Put this on your ear. It's bad."

Bart took the Kleenex from Kat and put pressure on his earlobe. "Thanks, Cous."

Aunt Rose said, "Here, let me take a look." She purveyed the deep slice, rifled through her purse, and came out with a butterfly bandage.

"And you wonder why I'm always prepared?" Ken asked Kat.

"Not anymore," Kat said.

Aunt Rose dug further into her purse and came out with alcohol wipes.

Chloe shook her head. "That's my mom. Never thought I'd appreciate her bottomless purse. But I do now."

Bart grimaced when Rose rubbed the alcohol into the gaping wound.

Rose applied the butterfly bandage, stood back, and appraised her work. "You'll have a scar, but you'll heal."

Rose turned to Chloe. "Why didn't you talk to me before you came here? What were you thinking?"

Chloe shrugged. "It's not like we've been on the best of terms, Mom. And I thought I'd catch a ghost or something. I didn't realize. . ."

"That's the problem. You don't think it through," Rose said. "Well, now we are here, we will have to survive until we can leave."

"I'll call Ranger Perez," Bart said. He picked up the satellite phone. "Huh, nothing. He said he would answer no matter what."

"Something isn't right," Ken said.

"Let's head back to the entrance. Maybe it's not really ringing through. The reception is better there," Kat said.

Rose walked toward the tripod and Shank's body.

"Mom? What are you doing?" Chloe asked.

Rose waved her away. "I want to look at something."

Bart walked up beside her. "You don't. We need to go as soon as possible."

"Give me a minute." Rose walked to the tripod and surveyed the pendant dangling from the center. "Oh my!"

"What?" Kat asked.

"Do you understand what is hanging there?" Rose asked as she pointed at the necklace.

"Not really."

"It is the Thorn of Christ." Rose turned on her heel, a look of shock and disbelief on her face.

"Ok. And . . .?" Ken asked.

"Legend has it one of the Roman soldiers took the thorn. As a trophy, sick though it was. He took it to a Roman glassmaker who encased it in glass. See the blue color of it? That's what Roman glass looked like. The soldier gave it to his wife as a gift. She was thrilled because she hated Jesus and saw it as a trophy. But when she put it on, it started to glow. It burned her. It is said she was never the same. She went insane and was dead within a year."

"That doesn't sound like Christ," Chloe said, "He's all kindness and love, right?"

"He is pure love. However, He is also the ultimate righteous judge of this world," Pastor Morton said. "He is holy and righteous. Maybe, just maybe, in His death, the crown took on some of His torment. An imprint, as it were, of the blackest day in history. And the judgment He took on for us carried over into the Crown of Thorns. What if the thorn can purge, even destroy, evil?"

"So why is it here?" Jet asked.

"That's the question of the hour. But where it sits tells me some-one wants it disabled. The sacrifice of your friend is an abomination of spiritual magnitude. Killing someone right beneath what may be a holy artifact—pure evil."

"Well, what should we do about it?"

"We need to release it and take it where it, and others, are safe."

"Mom. It's risky," Chloe said.

"If that's what it is purported to be, it's worth the risk," Rose replied.

"We can give it a try." Bart looked around the open field and spotted a long branch with two smaller limbs at one end, like a roughhewn meat fork. "This should do it."

Bart took the stick to the watery hole in the ground. "Sorry, guy," he said to Shank's corpse.

Bart stuck the twig out toward the chain. "Rats. It's too short. Hey, Melbourne, I can reach if you hold onto me, and I stretch all the way out."

"Not sure that's such a good idea, Brother," Ken said.

"You have a better way?"

Ken thought, shook his head, and walked over to Bart. "Let's hope I can hold you. Otherwise, you're joining our friend, and it won't be pretty."

"Roger that," Bart said.

Ken took hold of the belt loops on Bart's jeans. Thinking better of it, he took hold of the back of his waistband.

Bart leaned forward, stretching his long arms and the stick toward the medallion.

A blood-curdling scream forced Ken to jump backward. He dropped Bart.

Bart planted his palms in the dirt. His face hit the water. He sputtered and pushed himself backward away from the puddle. "Hey! What were you thinking?"

The shriek met his ears. Bart jumped up and ran toward the forest's edge.

"Someone is in trouble," Ken shouted.

"No kidding. We'll come back for the artifact. Let's find the owner of that scream."

––––––––––

Lucius stepped out from behind the tall trees into the clearing. Red Caps and blue sprites surrounded him.

"They almost got the artifact," he roared. He raised a finger. Electric light shot out. A fairy sizzled and dropped to the ground.

"If you worthless minions don't want the same fate, find and destroy them."

CHAPTER 28

The group trudged through the undergrowth toward the Witch House. Kat jogged ahead. "It sounded closer to the entrance," she said.

"Kat, slow down. We need to wait for Aunt Rose," Ken shouted.

Kat turned on her heel and walked back to Ken. "I'm sorry. Where is she?"

"I'm right here," Rose said. Pastor Morton held her elbow and helped her step over the low vegetation onto the road.

Rose brushed her dress and started toward Chloe.

A blood-curdling yell broke the conversation.

"It's not coming from the Witch House—it's coming from the Spider House we found the first day," Bart said.

Ken and Bart took off to a narrow dirt lane close to the entrance, turned right, and jogged toward the web.

"Oh, that's creepier than the Witch House. And that's hard to outdo," Jet said.

"What's inside isn't too pleasant either," Ken answered.

"For the love of Mike, PLEASE stay here," Ken said to the small clan but kept his eyes on Kat.

"Fine," Kat said.

Bart and Ken sneaked toward the entrance and disappeared inside.

Jet started to follow.

Bart held up his hand. "Not you."

"I know. Stay here and protect the others," Jet said.

"Exactly," Bart replied.

Chloe looked to her left, cocked her head, and walked to the trail's edge. "More drag marks?"

Kat walked up beside her, followed by Jet.

Deep grooves marked the dirt pathway, giving way to crushed grass, heading into the deeper foliage.

"Sure are. And, I hate to ask, but is that blood?" Kat looked down at the tall grass. Some of it was stained by dark red splotches.

"It does," Jet said.

"Ken," Kat shouted.

Ken and Bart came out of the Spider House. "What?"

"Over here," Kat said.

"Oh, man." Ken bent down and picked up a satellite phone. "Explains no answer."

"This does not bode well for Ranger Perez—or us," Bart said.

"We better find him." Ken started toward the woods.

"Not without me, FBI," Kat walked up beside him.

"I can't take you all. This is a possible crime scene, and we are already interfering with it."

"I don't think there'll be a police officer here for a long time," Rose said.

"Why not?"

"Well, first, we need to call them. But, second, they don't like this place any more than other residents of the area."

"If we tell them someone is injured, will they come?"

"Yes. But not after dark. And, we are getting toward dark—again."

"Kat. You make the call. And tell them about Shank, too. The rest of you stay put and out of trouble," Ken said.

"I'm more concerned about you. We have a prayer warrior and pastor here," Kat answered.

"And me," Jet said.

"And Jet. What are you doing for protection?" Chloe asked.

Bart took the brass bell from his pocket and rang it.

"It's a start," Kat said.

Rose dug into her purse and pulled out a small book. "Here. It's the New Testament. Use it!"

Ken took the small brown book and smiled. "Thanks, Aunt Rose."

Rose jerked her head at him, "Get going and be back here before it's dark."

"Yes, ma'am."

Ken and Bart made their way into the trees.

"Man, this stuff is denser than any I have ever seen in Alaska," Bart said.

"This place is like a rainforest. Things grow at record speed," Ken replied.

Ken pushed some low-hanging ivy to one side. They continued to follow the tracks.

"What is this?" Bart picked up a Black needle-like spike.

"If I didn't know better, I'd say it's from of spider. Do you remember the fuzzy stuff they have on their legs?"

"There's no arachnid this big in the world."

"I know. Weird."

They continued through the woods, batting mosquitos and pushing through the heavy growth.

"What do we have here?" Bart walked to his left. "Oh, man. I think I found part of the ranger."

Ken joined Bart. His shoulders sagged. He looked at the tan-colored object on the ground. A human nail was attached to it, and blood encircled it. "It's a finger. What predator are we up against?"

"I'm not sure," Bart said.

"Well, he could still be alive." Ken scrutinized the drag marks to his right. "Let's follow the tracks."

Ken released his gun.

Bart did the same.

The deep grooves ended at a small opening in some rocks.

"This looks like a part of the falls," Ken commented.

Bart cocked his head and listened. "I can hear water. I wonder if there's another way out of this accursed place."

"No time to find out. I think the ranger may be inside," Ken said.

Bart inhaled. "No time like the present to find out."

CHAPTER 29

Kat punched *End* on her cell phone and shook her head.

"Well?" Jet asked.

"Well, at first, the officer didn't believe me. But after I gave a few more details, he listened and said all officers are out on calls."

"Not acceptable. AT ALL." Aunt Rose held her hand out to Kat and wiggled her fingers. "The phone."

"Who are you going to call?"

"My friend, Author Trumball. You remember him, right? He was the judge who helped you with a license to marry."

"Right," Kat said.

"He can find us some help. And, he will believe me." Rose dialed.

"If anyone can bring help here, it would be Judge Trumball," Cloe whispered.

"Why?" Kat asked.

"You met him. He pretty much owns the town. He is both loved—and feared—by the residents. No one wants to cross him."

"He and I aren't on the best of terms. You don't have to mention I'm here, right?" Jet asked.

Rose scowled at Jet. "If you'd clean up your life, Jethro, you'd have much less anxiety."

"I don't have anxiety."

Rose patted Jet's arm. "I won't mention you are here."

Kat shrugged. "Well, if he has so much pull, having him in our corner is good."

Rose handed Kat her phone. "Arthur is on it. They should be on the way."

"Can they get in?"

"They can cut the chain if needed," Rose said.

"Ok. Let's go after Bart and Ken," Jet said.

"How will the officers know where to find us?" Chloe asked.

"Good point. Aunt Rose and Pastor Morton, would you stay by the gate?" Kat asked.

"If you give me a good reason. Maybe," Rose said.

"Ken would have my hide if you got any closer to danger than this," Kat said.

"We will stay," Pastor said. "We can do more good praying than fighting at our age."

"Thank you."

Kat scrutinized the long marks dotted with blood. The screech of a Red-Tailed Hawk reached her ears.

"It's looking for prey," Jet said.

"I think something else is looking for a kill, too, and it isn't human." Kat stepped onto the path.

Chloe stepped in behind her. "If there is a God, I pray He shows up now."

CHAPTER 30

Lucius stood beside the tripod, tapping his chin, lost in thought.
Burkist sailed up to his face.

Lucius batted at the fairy. "Back up, you smell foul."

Burkist chortled. "It is a wonderful scent. One of death and blood."

"What have you found?"

"Two have made it to the cave. They are inside."

"Did they find Mildred?"

"No. She took a human."

"She did? Why aren't you watching her, as I commanded? Now there is reason for more humans to come here!" Lucius roared.

Burkist hovered out of Lucius's reach.

Lucius pointed at Burkist. "Give me one good reason I shouldn't destroy you—and your entire army—this minute!"

"You need us. Without my army, you will not win against these humans. They have the One with them. You are vulnerable."

Lucius stared at the Red Cap leader. "There are many others who can help me."

"Yes, but it will take too long for them to arrive. We are here."

Lucius narrowed his eyes. "You have one more chance. STOP THE HUMANS. NOW."

Burkist bowed.

"If you do not achieve victory, I will hunt you and your entire clan down and destroy you."

Lucius stared at the aqua-blue glass floating above the bottomless hole in the ground. "I need to find someone to take this away and hide it," he whispered.

"Blue fairies, come!"

Cormorant swooped into the glade. "We are here."

"Guard the artifact with your lives."

CHAPTER 31

K at whirled around. "We need to grab the necklace."

"Why?" Chloe asked

"Because if it is as powerful as your Aunt Rose says, it may be the only thing to stop whatever is murdering people."

"What about Ken and Bart?" Jet asked.

"What can we do to help them? We can act as a diversion if we are lucky. Otherwise, we could be walking into a trap with no defense. Maybe the artifact is THE defense."

"Point taken. Let's go." Chloe turned and dashed back to the Spider House. She emerged onto the trail, Kat right behind.

"I thought you were going after Ken and Bart," Rose said.

"I thought you were going to the entrance," Chloe said.

"We are. But it will be a bit before help arrives, and we decided to pray over this area before moving on."

"It couldn't hurt," Kat said.

"So why are you back so soon?" Pastor Morton asked.

"Whoever, or whatever, put the ornament in the meadow thinks it's powerful enough to guard and kill for."

"It could be dangerous," Rose said.

"It may be dangerous to *not* retrieve it," Jet replied.

"True. Then we go with you," the Pastor said.

"Why? What can you do?" Chloe asked.

"Certain fairies hate the Bible, as you know; we can read verses. Does anyone have a bell?"

Chloe reached into her jacket pocket, pulled out a brass bell, and shook it. "Like this? Before you ask, I added it to my collection of things to take on a paranormal investigation. In fact, I have several." She handed bells to Kat, Jet, Rose, and Pastor Morton.

"To the clearing," Jet said, marching up the rough dirt lane.

"The silence here is deafening," Rose remarked.

A slight buzzing, like flies, started in the distance and grew steadily louder.

Kat threw her hands over her ears. She spotted a Red Cap flying toward them, followed by at least 50 more. "Start reading your Bible, Pastor!"

Pastor Morton started reading Psalm 91, "He that dwelleth in the secret place of the Most High shall abide under the shadow of the Almighty."

"Louder," Kat shouted. "They're still coming."

Pastor's voice boomed through the open field, "I will say of the LORD, He is my refuge and my fortress: my God; in him will I trust. Surely he shall deliver thee from the snare of the fowler, and from the noisome pestilence. He shall cover thee with his feathers, and under his wings shalt thou trust: his truth shall be thy shield and buckler. Thou shalt not be afraid for the terror by night; nor for the arrow that flieth by day; Nor for the pestilence that walketh in darkness; nor for the destruction that wasteth at noonday. A thousand shall fall at thy side, and ten thousand at thy right hand; but it shall not come nigh thee. Only with thine eyes shalt thou behold and see the reward of the wicked. Because thou hast made the LORD, which is my refuge, even the Most High, thy habitation; There shall no evil befall thee, neither shall any plague come nigh thy dwelling. For He shall give His angels charge over thee, to keep thee in all thy ways. They shall bear thee up in their hands, lest thou dash thy foot against a stone. Thou shalt tread upon the lion and adder: the young lion and the dragon shalt thou trample under feet. Because he hath set his love upon Me, therefore will I deliver him: I will set him on high, because he hath known My Name. He shall call upon Me, and I will answer him: I will be with him in trouble; I will deliver him, and honor him. With long life will I satisfy him, and shew him My salvation."

The red-hatted army picked up speed.

"Why isn't this working?" Chloe asked.

"I don't know," Kat said. "But, RUN."

Chloe, Kat, and Jet raced toward the trees.

"Wait." Chloe ran back to her mother, "Come on, Mom. You gotta go. Pastor, you too."

Rose stumbled and fell to her knees. "I can't, Chloe. Please run, and don't worry about me."

"I'm not leaving you here," Chloe said.

"She's not alone. I'm with her," Pastor Morton said.

"I'm not leaving you alone, either," Jet said. He took hold of the Pastor's elbow and guided him forward.

Chloe lifted Rose to her feet. "Come on."

Kat felt the wind of a wing as a Red Cap darted past her to block the exit to the forest. Several more soared to the forest's edge, making a living wall eight feet high.

"This may not end well," Kat breathed. She remembered all the times she had fought and won against demons and evil entities. *Maybe this time is the end*, she thought.

"God, if you are there, please get Chloe, Rose, and the Pastor out of here to safety," Kat prayed. "And, give me strength, no matter Your will for me."

The dusky light of the glade brightened into a familiar blue hue.

Uriel stood between the small team and the opening. He nodded at Kat.

Raphael stood at their rear.

Two more angels appeared, creating a blinding box of light around the assembly.

"Who dares to enter my domain?" A voice boomed from the tree line.

Uriel turned toward the voice. "The angels of the Most High God," he replied.

Lucius took a step into the glade. "You think you can defeat me?"

Uriel leveled his gleaming sword at Lucius. A white light shot from it toward the Red Caps between Uriel and Lucius. Several Red Caps burst into yellow-red flames and vanished. "Yes, I believe I can defeat you." He leveled the sword at Lucius.

Raphael pointed his sword at the Red Caps. It, too, sent out bright light, so brilliant Kat shut her eyes and turned her head to the side to avoid the glare.

The gate of Red Caps exploded into red and yellow flames, then vanished.

"I may not be able to kill you, Lucius, but I can bind you," Uriel said.

Shining bronze chains materialized in Uriel's hand. He threw the chains in the air and pointed them at Lucius.

Lucius turned and ran for the towering trees. The chains caught him before he escaped.

Lucius growled, then howled as the chains turned white hot and sizzled when the links touched his skin.

Lucius transformed from a human into a large, leather-winged being.

"A demon," Kat said. "How did I not know?"

"Why would you, Kat?" Rose asked.

"Demons exist?" Chloe said.

"For that matter, angels exist?" Jet said.

"Well, yeah. I didn't understand there were as many demons as there are. They are everywhere," Kat whispered.

Uriel turned and said, "You must take the artifact. It is the only way to save your friends."

The angels disappeared.

Pastor Morton fell to his knees and looked up. "Thank you, Lord." He got up and started toward the tripod.

A loud whirring advanced toward the clearing.

"What now?" Rose asked.

"I'd say we have more fairies to contend with."

Kat turned to pinpoint the whereabouts of a low, droning buzz. The blue sprites glided into the meadow.

"You're kidding, right? Didn't you see Lucius get roped and destroyed? Or were you on break?" Kat asked.

"We have been given a mission; we will complete it," Perse said.

"Love your determination," Chloe said. "But you guys are wimps compared to your big cousins." She raised the brass bell in her hand and shook. The melodious chime echoed all around them. Kat, Jet, Rose, and the Pastor followed Chloe, ringing their brass bells until the sound flooded the meadow.

The blue fairies howled, covered their ears, and somersaulted out of the glade.

"And good riddance," Chloe said.

Kat picked up the stick Bart had used earlier.

She dropped to her stomach and inched forward, working to ignore Shank's decaying corpse. She wrinkled her nose and held her breath, stretching her arm toward the aquamarine glass. She touched the chain, just missing it.

Chloe looked around. "I can't find anything to help."

"Let me try," Jet said.

"Thank you." Kat retreated from the stench of Shank's death and handed the stick to Jet.

"Grab his feet," Rose said.

Kat took Jet's left foot, and Chloe took his right foot.

"Now try," Rose said.

Pastor Morton walked up beside Jet. He glanced at the decaying corpse. "May you rest in peace," he muttered.

Jet inched forward until his chest rested on the rim of the water hole. Dirt and rock gave way under his weight.

"Jesus help us," Pastor Morton murmured.

Jet's arm shot out toward the pendant.

The stick hooked it.

Jet threw it over his shoulder.

Chloe jumped and caught the necklace midair.

"Thank you, Jesus," Pastor said.

Chloe scrutinized the thorn surrounded by blue-green glass. "It sure looks like a thorn."

"Put it in a pocket you can zip," Kat said. "No matter what it is or isn't, the evil ones don't want us to have it."

"How about you take it?" Chloe held the chain out to Kat.

Kat gave Chloe a questioning look.

"Well, I don't want to be responsible for something like this."

"I'll take it," Jet offered.

Kat snatched the pendant. "Thanks, just the same, Jet. I'll feel safer if I hold onto it. Let's go." Kat sprinted out onto the pathway.

CHAPTER 32

Ken blinked, waiting for his eyes to adjust to the darkness. He sniffed and threw a hand over his nose.

Bart unbelted his flashlight. The beam bounced off wet rock walls several feet into the cave. He scanned the area. "There!" He trotted to a heap of khaki-brown clothing in the middle of the cavern.

Ken bent down and rolled Ranger Perez to his back. He checked for a pulse. "Believe it or not, he's still alive."

Bart shook his head. He took in a hand, missing a finger, still bleeding from the wound. The ranger's face was covered in deep scratches. His side had puncture wounds, oozing blood. "But for how long? He has some nasty injuries."

"What do you think did this?" Ken asked.

"I've seen bear maulings less brutal," Bart said. "Maybe a Mountain Lion?"

Ken pulled up the ranger's shirt. "These aren't teeth marks." He pointed to the rounded holes, seeping red liquid. A massive welt, inflamed with infection, surrounded the two circular wounds.

"Man, if I didn't know better, I'd say it's a spider bite. Or a snake," Bart said.

"Whatever did this, it's big."

Bart released his gun from his belt and held it toward the ground.

Ken did the same.

Bart shined the light around the cave. "Let's find out where this goes." He stepped toward an opening to the left.

"Woah." Ken held his arm. "We need to help Ranger Perez."

"Let's move him out of the cave and bind his wounds as best we can. Help is supposed to be on the way."

Ken and Bart lifted the ranger. Ken took the lead. They emerged from the cave.

Bart took off his jacket and laid it on the ground.

They positioned Perez under a tree. Ken dug through his backpack and pulled out an emergency medical kit. He applied antiseptic to the wounds and covered them with gauze. He bound the hand missing its finger in more gauze. "That's about all I can do for him."

Bart and Ken twirled and faced the underbrush.

Ken held his gun level. "Come out, now. And no fast moves," he commanded.

Kat emerged from the foliage, hands in the air. "I come in peace."

Ken lowered his gun. "You could have gotten yourself killed."

Kat took in Bart and Ken, guns now at their sides. She scanned the area and saw the opening in the rock, then the ranger. "Oh!"

Chloe, Jet, Rose, and Pastor Morton strolled into the open area.

"This man needs help," Rose hurried over to the ranger.

"Aren't the police on the way, Aunt Rose? Can't they help?"

"They are."

"Then, the only thing left is to sit with him until help gets here."

Ken and Bart took off for the cave.

"Where do you think you're going?" Kat asked.

"To find what did this to him," Bart replied.

"I have grave concerns," Chloe said. "Whatever did this to him may not be normal."

"Why do you think such a thing?"

"Because the Lucius legend mentions someone named Mildred. And she is to be protected at all costs for some reason. What if this Mildred isn't a person?"

Bart lifted his gun toward the sky. "That's why we have these."

"And what if they don't work?"

"Look. If we can't get through the gate for some reason, we need to find another way out of this horrid little amusement park. We heard water and think there is another way out beside the falls. We are going in to find it. Whatever did this to him is probably long gone."

Kat glared at Ken. "And if it's not?"

Ken shrugged. "We will think of something."

Bart and Ken continued toward the cave.

"And, all of you stay here." Ken turned and faced Kat. "I especially mean you!"

Kat stood silent.

Bart slapped Ken's shoulder. "Let's go."

Ken nodded and took off behind Bart, ducking through the opening in the boulders.

"Do you think she'll listen?" Ken asked Bart.

"Nope."

"Me, either."

They headed over to the opening.

"I don't see anything but black," Ken said.

Bart stepped into a rocky corridor. Water dripped and echoed through the area, sounding like a firecracker exploding with each drop.

Ken and Bart walked single file until the corridor opened into a large, two-story room.

A circle of leaves, limbs, and dirt stood in the middle of the room. It rose about five feet high.

"Ideas of the reason for the mess in the middle here?" Ken asked.

"It looks like a nest."

"Great. What would build it?"

"I'd say an enormous bird."

"Well, I've never seen a bird cover its nest in that." Bart pointed to the outward white tendrils binding the dirt and foliage.

A loud hiss, followed by a banshee-like scream, filled the room, echoing from the walls.

Bart turned.

Ken shined a light around and up the rocks.

A large, fur-covered being stared down at the two through glittering blue eyes.

"Those eyes are so large I think I can see my reflection in them," Ken whispered to Bart.

"You think this is Mildred?" Bart asked.

"I'd venture a guess," Ken said.

The thing jumped to ground level and rushed the duo.

Bart raised his gun and leveled it at the creature. The ricochet of the bullet almost deafened him.

"That didn't work. Now what?" Ken asked.

Mildred lumbered forward.

Ken and Bart dove under the nest. Fluid dripped in a steady stream from it to the floor around them.

Ken snuck toward the unprotected area. A large, barbed appendage shot out from Mildred.

"Hey, Ugly Spider, over here!"

"I knew she wouldn't stay put," Ken said.

Bart scrambled out from under the nest, running to get between Kat and Mildred.

The black spider snatched up Kat and lifted her in the air.

"Let me down, you ugly thing!"

Something sounding like a maniacal laugh surrounded Kat.

"I don't think so," It hissed. "I'm hungry. You will do."

Chloe ran into the room. Her eyes grew wide when she saw the monster holding Kat several feet in the air.

It swiped at Chloe, grazing her leg before she dove under the nest to safety.

"I told you to stay put," Ken said.

"We need to free Kat," Chloe said.

Ken scanned the area, looked up, and saw a thicker tree limb hanging by a white string. He yanked. The tree limb gave way. "We need something flammable."

"Here." Bart pulled a pocket knife from his jeans, cut a strip from Ken's shirt, then his own.

"How do we light it?"

"I've got it," Cloe said. She pulled a Bic lighter from her pocket.

"We need something to get it started—and fast," Bart said.

Mildred drew Kat closer to its clawed mouth.

Chloe lifted the still-lit Bic lighter to the top of the torch. The flame caught fire on a silken thread above her. Chloe spun the sticky strings around the homemade torch like she was creating cotton candy. "This will work." She lit it.

Ken took hold of the firebrand and ran toward Mildred. He placed the fire on the spider's leg. It screeched and dropped Kat, turning to Ken.

Ken ran for the nest, grabbing Kat on the way.

"Ok, thanks for your help, FBI," Kat said.

"I told you to stay put."

"I can't let you out of my sight. Look at the trouble you're in now," Kat retorted.

"What's going on in your pocket?" Bart asked.

Kat looked down. The left front pocket of her jacket glowed. She unzipped it and pulled out the necklace.

Everyone gathered closer when the glow went from a dull white light to blinding. The wood inside the glass was on fire, yet the wood itself seemed untouched.

Mildred attacked the nest, tearing apart leaves and limbs.

"It's going to come down on us. We have to get out now," Ken barked.

They dove to the opposite side of the nest, away from Mildred, and scooched out.

Kat put the chain around her neck and inched toward the hallway, others in front, Ken to her side. She scanned the room to locate Mildred.

Mildred was almost on them, its long legs taking three to five steps for each step of theirs.

Kat turned again. The thorn in the blue glass glowed brighter.

Mildred shrieked and retreated to the opposite side of the cave.

Kat looked at the pendant, then at Mildred. "You don't like this, huh? Well, you know what? I don't like you." Kat yanked the pendant from her neck and ran toward Mildred.

"What are you doing?" Ken raced after her.

"I'm ridding us of this thing once and for all. I don't like being considered someone's next meal. In fact, I don't want *anyone* to be the next meal."

Mildred recoiled and crouched low, and sprang for the high ledge.

"No, you don't," Chloe ran at the spider and smacked its back leg with the torch.

Mildred screeched and whirled on Chloe.

Kat slid to a stop beside Chloe and held up the pendant.

Mildred backed up against the wall.

Kat inched closer. "What do I do with this now?" She whispered.

"If it is the Thorn of Christ, it will destroy the evil it touches," Chloe said.

"How do I put it on her? She isn't going to volunteer for self-destruction."

"True," Chloe dug into her bag and pulled out a metal camp fork. She dug further and came out with a rubber band.

"What are you thinking?" Kat asked.

"We can make a slingshot." Chloe scoured the floor and found a large leaf. She wound the rubber band through it and attached it to the camp fork.

Kat dropped the pendant into the sling. "Jesus, if You are here, please aim this thing."

Kat pulled back and released the pendant.

It soared to the left of Mildred, and then like an invisible hand batted it back, the pendant turned and flew toward the spider's chest.

Mildred screeched and crumpled to the ground. All eight legs shriveled beneath her. The black fur on Mildred's chest sizzled, then glowed as the pendant seemed to dissolve into its torso.

Bart, Ken, Kat, and Chloe stared in disbelief as Mildred continued to wither. Smoke from her wound filled the area.

The mist cleared, and a young woman lay in a pile of ash.

"What have we done?" Kat ran to the girl.

The girl smiled at Kat. "Thank you," she said through labored breaths.

"Who are you?"

"My name used to be Millie. I was human, like you. My father swore an oath to Lucius because he couldn't stand my dying. So, Lucius promised him I would live if my father and I agreed to his terms. We did. And I became what you saw."

"Where are those paramedics?" Kat said over her shoulder.

"They aren't here yet," Ken said.

"We need to help her!"

"No, you don't. My time is over. I am praying God forgives me. I am dying. And, I am thankful to be free of the monster I had become."

Pastor Morton walked to Millie. "Do you believe in Jesus Christ?"

"I did," she said.

"Do you now?"

Mildred's dark eyes met the Pastor's. She smiled. "Yes, I believe I do."

"Then you will be in paradise with Him today."

Mildred smiled and went limp.

"No!" Kat said. "She deserves a life."

"She will have a life. Better than you can imagine," Pastor Morton said.

The young woman Kat cradled, jerked, became a skeleton, and dissolved into dust.

"What just happened?" Kat asked.

"She was past the time of her natural death. She is free now."

Kat shook her head. "Evil never ceases to amaze me. And people doing evil in the name of good really never ceases to amaze me."

Ken helped Kat to her feet. He drew her close for a hug. "I love you, Katrina Melbourne."

"Even though I don't do as you say?"

"Even then." Ken kissed the top of her head.

"As they say, get a room!" Chloe said.

"Let's get out of here," Bart said.

EPILOGUE

The emergency vehicles ' blue and red flashing lights grew smaller in the distance and vanished.

Kat turned to Ken. "Well, that went better than expected."

"It did. Weren't we fortunate to find a way out?"

"I'd say God showed us the way out," Rose said. "There is no way we would have found the opening unless Millie, God rest her soul, had not stopped right there."

"Yes, Aunt Rose," Ken said.

"It was neat and tidy," Bart said. "We didn't have to explain a skeleton in the cave. The ranger is getting help and is better. Unfortunately, they are still looking for Shank's killer, but I don't think they will find the perpetrator."

"Not unless they run into a demon who was sent back to hell or those weird pixies who seemed to disappear when he did," Jet said.

Ken's phone chirped. He held up a finger to Kat and walked off.

"Well, all's well that ends well," Rose smiled.

Ken snapped his phone shut and returned to his friends.

Kat looked into his eyes. "Well?"

Ken sighed. "We've been asked to investigate a string of murders in South Carolina."

"Ken, I want to go home! I want to go back to Ravens Cove!"

"And we will. Right after we help. These are young kids who are going missing. How could I say no?"

"And why do they need you and me?"

"Right before the kids go missing, they start speaking in an unfamiliar voice, and there is a monk, not a priest, a monk who always befriends them and before the disappearance."

"And?"

"And, rumor has it this monk happens to have red glowing eyes and talons for fingers."

Kat's shoulders slumped. "After this one, right, we go home?"

"Yes, after this one."

The End

www.ingramcontent.com/pod-product-compliance
Lightning Source LLC
Chambersburg PA
CBHW071128250626
47159CB00006B/2175